MURDER BY NUMBERS

AN ADDIE FOSTER MYSTERY

BOOK 3

Kimberley O'Malley

Carolina Blue
PUBLISHING

WHERE ROMANCE IS TRUE BLUE & RED HOT!

Published by Carolina Blue Publishing, LLC

Copyright 2019, Carolina Blue Publishing, LLC

ISBN: 978-1-946682-15-4

For my super stalkers, I mean readers. I am so very thankful for your continued appreciation for and support of my books. It makes all the self-doubt vanish when I hear how much you enjoyed reading one of my books. You know who you are. More importantly, I know who you are.

Praise for
Kimberley O'Malley

Death Comes in Threes

"This was my first cozy mystery and I have to say I absolutely loved it. Kimberley did an amazing job at keeping me guessing what was coming next. I can't wait to see what happens between Addy and Detective Wolfe cause something has to happen between them! I also want to know who the man in Addy's dream is. And why those men were after her. Can't wait for the next book!"

-Under Cover Book Blog

"This was the first Cozy Mystery and Kimberley knocked it out of the park. I loved Addie and Grey and the two aunties. The detective puts out the vibe he is serious and hard core. But I am sure he has a soft spot for Addie. Hopefully in the next book we will see where the sparks fly for Addy and why these guys were after her. KUDOS to Kimberley for such a great read."

-Wanda Bridget Hickey, Verified Kindle customer

"This was my first Cozy Mystery and I loved it. I was drawn in by Addie and adored Grey. He was such a charming, funny and protective character. I can't wait to find out more in book two.

This book is great for rainy days or a light read while you're on holiday."

-Author T. S. Petersen

Dyeing for Change

"Love Addie mysteries, but hate that they are such a quick read. And that I have to wait for the next one!"

-Amazon certified customer.

"Another action-packed book. Don't let it being short stop you from reading. You will absolutely love Addie and her BFF, Grey. They're hilarious. Can't forgot our hottie detective, Jonah. Meow! Trouble is always finding our Addie. She doesn't listen, at all, even if it's for her own good. She loves her dogs, and this book made me shed some tears because of one of her dogs. You can't go wrong with this awesome book. Read the first and then come devour the second."

-Sara, Amazon Kindle customer

"I am really liking this series! A nice, easy and quick read - just enough to take a break from real life and spend a lazy hour or so with a good read. Likeable characters and a continuing mysterious thread involving the main character throughout the two books so far - looking forward to seeing what happens in Book #3!"

-Vivian F. Shane, Amazon Kindle customer

Chapter One

Addie Foster lay on her side, hands bound in front of her. Course rope bit into her ankles. An old, musty cloth had been tied around her mouth to ensure her silence. She pulled on the rope surrounding her wrists, hoping for some leeway. No such luck; the bonds tightened with her struggle.

The door to the room opened, and she closed her eyes. Better for them to think she was still out from the drug they'd used earlier. They spoke in whispers, as if unsure whether she could hear them. She strained to hear but could only make out their voices, not actual words. The tone, however, sent icy shivers down her spine.

The obnoxious blaring of her alarm dragged Addie from the nightmare. She lay in bed, heart pounding. But not only from the dregs of the nightmare that remained. The vague, lingering feeling of doom bothered her more. Ever since suffering a concussion last spring, she'd been prone to weird, often prophetic dreams.

Never could contain lottery numbers though, could they?

She grabbed her phone to shut off her alarm. And then scrolled to her calendar. Estate sale day! Excitement replaced worry. Gracey & Lily, her two Shelties, looked up from their bed on the floor. Both yawned and stretched before pouncing on her feet as she swung them out of bed.

"Someone didn't have any nightmares, I see. Let's go out!"

With those words, the dogs became grey and black streaks, yipping and chasing each other to the kitchen slider. She followed at a slower pace, opening it and releasing them into her fenced back yard. The chilly morning air nibbled at her bare toes.

After pouring some juice and promising herself a large coffee on the way, she slid a bagel into the toaster and waited. Her phone came alive with the sound of a shrieking ghost, Grey's idea of Halloween humor. Her BFF loved the holiday and had been ramping up all month.

"Good morning, friend. You're up early for a Saturday. I'm not leaving for over an hour." She loved her Saturday adventures into old homes and estates; Grey, not so much. Dragging him at the crack of dawn, as she would have preferred, was out of the question.

"About that..."

"You promised!" Between his significant other, Jamie, and her budding relationship with Jonah, their pal time had taken a hit.

"It's not that I don't want to go traipsing through musty old houses on the off chance of finding a first edition Dickens. And I can hear you rolling your eyes."

She laughed. "You can't hear someone roll their eyes. But I am, by the way. Good guess."

"Not a guess. Just over twenty-five years of knowing you. But I have a reason this time. Erin called me. She's not feeling well. Not sure if it's viral or too much partying on campus last night, but she's not coming in this morning. That leaves me to hold down the fort."

Erin McCarthy, their not quite full-time help, studied English full-time at the University of North Carolina in nearby Wilmington.

"She's not really the partying type. I'll go with something viral."

"Doesn't matter. I'll be here, and not with you."

"You don't have to sound so happy about it."

"I'll miss you, but no, I won't miss that. You can always take Detective Hottie with you. He has nothing but free time these days."

"Not nice, Grey. Especially since you and I are the reason he got shot." Addie shuddered remembering those terrifying hours when she waited outside the operating room.

"My bad. Anyway, maybe he'll go with you."

"Not sure it's his thing."

"He's allowed to defer, and I'm not? Hardly seems fair."

"I *like* him," she said with a laugh.

"You *love* me."

"True. But you know how it is. This thing between us is new. I don't want to rush it."

"You mean have him find out you're a big geek."

"That, too." She sighed. "I really like him, Grey."

"I know you do, honey. And he really likes you. But this isn't the usual start to a relationship, now is it?"

"There is that."

They'd first met in July, when she stumbled across a dead body in her neighborhood, and Jonah thought she might have killed the guy. She went from suspect to potential next victim in the blink of an eye, when the victim turned out to be a wanted criminal from Eastern Europe. Two of his goons tried to kill her, each meeting a sudden and violent end. She still had no idea why.

"How's he feeling, by the way? Is he bored out of his mind yet? Wearing something other than a dark suit?"

"Funny. No suits in physical therapy. He never complains. Pushes himself."

More than six weeks ago, her life had turned on its axis again when she witnessed her friend's murder. Jonah had ended up on the wrong side of the bad guy's gun, trying to save her. And Grey.

"Have you had your third date yet?" He didn't even try to hide his laughter. That was his code for had they slept together yet.

"The man took a bullet. For me. Some respect wouldn't kill you, you know."

"Exactly my point. He saved your life. The least you could do is give him a little something."

"I am *not* discussing my sex life with you. No matter how much I love you. Talk to you later."

She disconnected on his laughter. They hadn't gone there yet, not that he needed to know. Jonah had been shot once, the bullet traveling through his upper arm, wreaking havoc along its path. A nicked artery and fractured humerus had required emergent surgery - while she emptied the vending machine and waited.

Two pair of bright eyes appeared at the slider, followed quickly by yet more nose art, as she referred to the smudges the girls left behind. "I'm coming. Hold your fur." She let them in and watched as they ran to their empty dishes. One looked more pathetic than the other. "Who's hungry?" As expected, the words set off a hurricane of activity. Both dogs raced around her heels.

Addie poured food into each bowl before giving them fresh water. Chuckling as they attacked their food, she left the kitchen to take a shower. Too early to call Jonah. Since being on extended leave, he'd enjoyed sleeping like a "real person", as he called it. She'd let him rest.

Thirty minutes later, showered, dressed, and itching to get going, Addie let the girls out one more time. As she waited for them to do their business, the opening chords of "Thriller", another of Grey's jokes, sounded from her phone.

Jonah!

Sensation zinged through her. She grabbed her phone, sliding a finger across the screen.

"Hey, good morning. You're up early."

"But you sound like you've been up way longer."

His sleep-roughened voice sent a frisson of sensation down her spine.

"Maybe an hour. Just heading out the door in a few." She walked to the glass door and opened it to let the girls back in.

"Let me guess. Off to another estate sale. Nothing else puts that excitement in your voice."

"You do."

"Good to know. If only I had two good, working arms, I'd show you how I feel about you."

And the zings started in her toes and traveled all throughout her body. "Can I get a rain check on that?"

"Of course."

The sound of rustling sheets met her ear. She swallowed. Hard. And pictured him lying in bed. And then checked for drool.

"Ah, are you still in bed?"

"If I said yes, would you rush over?"

"Would you want me to?" She held her breath, pulse slamming in her throat, waiting for his answer.

"More than you know." He sighed. "How about a proper date? Where we go out to dinner, talk about our days."

"And no discussion of crime or suspects? I'd love that."

"I can't drive yet. Which means I can't pick you up. So, it won't be a strictly proper date."

"That's the best kind."

Chapter Two

Sunshine dappled across the country road. Leaves of varying shades of orange, red, and yellow tumbled in the breeze. Fall had arrived, and no one loved it more than Addie Foster. From the nip in the air to the pumpkin spiced everything, she was fall's number one fan.

Singing along to an oldie from Garth Brooks, with more enthusiasm than talent, she drove to the estate sale. Her GPS announced the final turn, down a long driveway with heavy woods on either side. Her smile grew as she drew closer to the sprawling house. She pulled to the side of it, squeezing in-between two pickup trucks. Cars and trucks of assorted sizes and shapes were parked at every angle.

Addie nodded to a few people she passed as she made her way to the front entrance. She approached a gentleman with a clipboard. "Good morning. I guess I missed the opening."

"Yes, ma'am, but only by a little bit."

"Is Claire working today?" She knew the company owner from having attended many of these events.

"I'm afraid Ms. Worthington is not. Is there something you're looking for? I can direct you."

"Books; the older, the better. I own a shop in Ocean Grove."

"Oh, then you've come to the right place. Mrs. Abernathy was a great reader. They both were, really, but the mister has been gone for more than ten years. Mr. Abernathy was also a bit of an adventurer, believed pirates buried treasure around here. Can you imagine? Never found so much as a gold doubloon. Didn't keep him from trying though."

"Really?" She laughed at the thought. "Well, a first edition in decent shape is my idea of treasure."

He held the door for her. "Then you'll want to head down the main hallway. Take the second door on the right. That's the library, ma'am. Hopefully, you'll find something that catches your fancy."

"Thank you, sir."

Addie headed inside, gasping at the foyer. A beautiful stairway rose majestically on each side before meeting at the top. Dark, gleaming wood paneled the way. She passed exquisite antique furniture, barely resisting the urge to trail her fingertips along the highly polished surfaces. Framed portraits in ornate, gold frames graced the walls.

Dreaming of what she'd find in the library hastened her steps. Double doors, left ajar, beckoned to her. She held her breath, sending out positive thoughts into the universe for a find. Not generally superstitious, Addie crossed her fingers before entering. She did it every time she attended a sale like this one.

A large, ornate marble fireplace dominated the room. Or would for most people. But the floor-to-ceiling bookshelves drew her eye. They made her want to skip with glee. A woman stood near the fireplace, holding a clipboard. Addie approached her.

"Good morning. Do you by any chance have an inventory of the books available? And are all the books in this room for sale?"

The older woman smiled, handing her several pages stapled together. "This is the most up to date list. I understand Mrs. Abernathy donated some things to local libraries. As you're the first one in the room this morning, I believe this should be current. Happy hunting."

"Thanks." She rubbed her hands together. "This should be great fun!"

Addie moved off when another person approached the woman. Glancing through the sheets, she made a check next to several items of interest to her. One of her Internet customers collected Victorian gardening books. There were two books by Jane Louden on her wish list. Addie dragged her finger down the alphabetical list, stopping when she found that exact name. She did a little happy dance in place. Not only were the two books she needed included, but a third as well. Maybe she could tempt Mrs. Henrietta Gavin of Rochester, New York.

The last page of the handout held a map of the room. She found the section she needed and headed there. The gardening books were in excellent condition. She placed all three books in the shoulder bag she brought for carrying her finds.

The next few hours passed as she perused the room, building quite a 'to buy' pile. As she negotiated prices with the woman, Addie spied several boxes of books piled in the corner.

"Are those part of the sale?"

The woman, Betty per her name tag, turned to look. "Oh, yes. They're not included in the inventory, as they were just discovered early this morning in the cellar." She leaned in and lowered her voice. "Between you and me, they're kind of an afterthought. Priced to sell, if you know what I mean. Twenty-five dollars per box."

"Let me take a look."

Addie walked over to them, grimacing at the thought of any books being doomed to a damp basement. Two contained mostly mass-market fiction in paperback. She passed over them. But a third held hard bound books. An older man in a tweed jacket approached the area. On impulse, she grabbed the last box. She didn't miss his frown as she turned back to Betty.

"I'll add this as well."

"Very good, ma'am. Will you need any assistance getting these to your car?"

Addie looked around her and laughed. "Might be a good idea."

Betty wrote up her purchases, to be paid in the foyer. She thanked her and gave her a description of her car. After paying, Addie continued outside, carrying the box of books. A young man brought the rest of them, placing the books in her car. She thanked him and turned to leave.

"Pardon me," sounded from behind her. Addie turned to see the tweed wearing gentleman standing behind her car.

She pushed her sunglasses to the top of her head. "Yes? May I help you?"

A smile spread across his face. But not a smile with any warmth behind it. "It's more about how I can help you." His English accent should have been charming.

She gripped the keys in her hand tighter. After the past few months, meetings with strange men, even in broad daylight with others milling about, spooked her. "I'm not sure what you mean."

"That last box of books you bought. I'd like to take it off your hands. For a profit, of course." His smile grew.

"No, thank you. Enjoy the rest of your day."

She started to turn away when he grabbed her arm. She turned back, pulling her arm from his grip.

"Name your price."

She took a step back, crossing her arms in front of her. "I said no, thank you." People who thought everyone had a price annoyed her.

"I'm sorry if I offended you. I'm just very interested in that box."

"There were several others available. I'm not selling. Good day."

Addie opened her car door and got in. As she closed the door, she swore she heard him mutter, "We'll see about that."

Addie reversed out of her space. He backed up only enough to let her by. A deep scowl replaced his earlier smile. He grew smaller in her rear-view mirror. The feeling of unease did not.

*****

That afternoon, Addie had mostly forgotten about the strange encounter. Mostly. She decided not to tell Grey or Jonah. No use worrying them about it.

After arriving back at the shop and breaking Grey for his lunch, she sat behind the counter, composing an email to the woman who collected the gardening books. Her fingers flew over the keys, excitement in every stroke. She couldn't wait to read the reply from Mrs. Henrietta Gavin of Rochester, New York. She hit send just as the little bell over the door announced a customer.

She turned her head, prepared to greet them. And zings of pleasure raced through her blood. "Jonah!" She jumped from her perch, racing around the corner of the counter. Gracey and Lily yipped from their shared dog bed.

He caught her in his good arm, kissing the top of her head. "That never gets old," he said with a huge smile.

She cocked her head. "What doesn't?"

"Hearing you call me something other than 'Detective'."

"Never gets old saying it either."

She stood back, holding him at arm's length. He looked thinner, paler than she liked. But all in all, seeing him on his feet made her heart happy.

"Do I pass inspection?"

"Always. But you've lost some weight. I worry about you."

He shook a finger at her. "Welcome to my world. But don't. I'm getting stronger every day."

She ignored the bell over the door. "I'd offer to fatten you up, but we both know that's not exactly my strong suit."

"That's putting it mildly," joked Grey, coming through the door.

"Very funny." She resisted sticking her tongue out at him. Barely. She turned back to Jonah. "How'd you get here? Please tell me you didn't drive." She pointed at his left arm, contained in a splint.

He shuffled his feet. "I, uh, called Grey."

"Guilty," the man in question agreed. He sailed into the store, stopping to kiss Addie on the cheek. "He lives close to lunch." He held up a take-out bag from Battalion Bar-B-Que.

Her mouth watered. "Hush puppies?"

"Well, duh. What's lunch from Battalion without hush puppies? Too bad I didn't get any for you though." He looked her up and down. "You'll thank me when your pants loosen."

Jonah leaned back against the counter, face straight but shoulders shaking.

Addie glared at him, then Grey. "That. Is. Not. Funny." And kept herself from checking her waistband.

Were they more snug than usual?

"You must have a death wish," Jonah muttered. "I think you look beautiful."

"Suck up," sniped Grey.

"Boys, that's enough."

Grey passed a container to her. "One side of greasy but delicious hush puppies."

She grabbed them before he changed his mind. "Did you get the...?" She stopped when he held up a finger.

"Requisite cinnamon butter?" He smirked. "I'm not an amateur."

"And now I remember why I love you."

"Oh, there are so many reasons. Where would you start?"

"I'm glad you're gay. Otherwise, I might worry you're trying to poach my girlfriend."

And something shifted in her chest. Something warm and gooey. "Is that what I am? Your girlfriend?" She didn't have to see the smile spreading across her face to know it was more than a little silly.

"Answer carefully," Grey advised.

"You shush."

"Well, I, uh, just thought…" The tips of Jonah's ears turned an alarming shade of red.

"Grey, why don't you take your lunch into my office?" Her tone made it clear it wasn't a question.

He gave her a snappy salute. "Yes, ma'am."

She took her hush puppies around the counter and sat on the stool. "I am an independent woman, clinging by my nails to thirty-four. I own my own business. I don't need a title, Jonah. We're cool."

He held her gaze while approaching the counter. Never looked away. "I have a few years on you, Addie, and I like titles. I want to tell people you're my girlfriend. Are you cool with that?"

She would have answered, but that required oxygen. So, she nodded.

"Good. How'd it go?"

Addie blinked. "Go?" Verbal whiplash at its best.

One corner of his mouth raised, displaying the dimple she obsessed over. "You know, the sale you attended." He pointed to the stacks of books surrounding her. "Looks like you found some stuff."

Two can play at this game.

"When you smile like that, raise one corner of your mouth, I want to kiss the dimple that appears. Have wanted to for a long time. Weeks now."

He leaned in so close, she watched his pupils turn from milk to dark chocolate. "Really? Tell me more."

Addie leaned in closer still. Licked her lips. Made sure she had his attention. "I found first editions of Jane Louden's *British Wildflowers.* Mrs. Henrietta Gavin of Rochester, New York, will be tickled."

Chapter Three

"We really need to go on that first date." A lock of his thick, dark hair fell into his eyes.

"Yeah, we do," she breathed. She reached out, brushed it back. And smiled. "I've wanted to do that for a while, too."

"There's something I've wanted to do for some time." He straightened and came around the counter. He took one of her hands with his good one. "This is not the way I wanted this to happen. Goodness knows, I've thought about it." He raised her hand to his mouth, turning it over, and kissed her palm.

Her knees liquified. Breath caught in her lungs.

He pulled her closer to him. "Thought about how your lips would taste."

"Hey, kids!"

They sprang apart like guilty teens. She fixed him with her best stare. Grey laughed.

"Dude, do you really want your first kiss to happen here? With spectators?"

Jonah hung his head. "He's always going to be here, isn't he?" he asked without any heat.

"Yep." This from Grey.

"He grows on you. Kind of like a fungus."

"Hey."

"I meant that in the best possible way."

Jonah sighed. "He's right though."

"I am? Oh, I am." He looked at Addie, then Jonah. "You really haven't kissed yet? What's taking you so long?"

Good question!

"He got shot. Remember?" Now that she knew he wanted to kiss her, had been thinking about kissing her, it was the only thing she could think of.

"Oh, yeah. Guess that might get in the way."

"It's not that I don't like you, Grey. But do we have to discuss everything with you?"

"Pretty much."

"No, we don't." She glared at him for a second time. With equally dismal results. "No, Jonah, we most definitely do not. In fact, why don't you and I go for a drive? Take in the sights?" She closed the lid of her laptop, tucking it into her backpack. Then she grabbed his good hand. "We're off."

"She's bossy like that sometimes."

Jonah grinned over his shoulder. "I know. I like it."

Addie whistled for the girls. "Who wants to go for a ride?"

Both dogs scrambled out of their bed, running to catch up with their mistress. At the back door, she stopped to snap on their leashes. She straightened to find him grinning at her.

"What?"

"We get to do something normal. Drive around. Look at the foliage. Like normal people." He held the door for her.

The man from the estate sale popped into her head. She'd thought about mentioning it to him. Not that he'd done anything particularly threatening. But coupled with the dream...no, not today.

"Yeah, normal. Who would have guessed?"

"Where are we going?" He grinned at her. "Not that it matters." He stepped back while she raised the back hatch. The girls jumped in and lay down.

"You say the loveliest things." She helped him fasten his seatbelt, ignoring the slightly clenched jaw. She soothed the bunched muscles with the stroke of a finger." I know you can do everything yourself, despite the arm in a splint and the too recent major surgery. I like to help."

And the clouds dissipated from his gaze. "I know you do. And I appreciate it."

"Once more with feeling, maybe. Before you know it, you won't need me for anything."

She started to close the door when he grabbed her hand. "I'll need you."

"Okay, then." She shut his door and remembered to breathe.

*****

Twenty minutes later, Addie turned down a rutted lane off the country road. She lowered her speed to lessen the jostling to his arm.

"Sorry. It'll be worth it, I promise."

"I trust you," he ground out through gritted teeth.

Slowing the car to a crawl, she inched her way down the path. They emerged from the trees and pulled to a stop in front of a farmhouse. A huge apple orchard surrounded it on three sides.

"Ta da. We're here."

A chorus of excited yips sounded from the back.

"Hold on, girls. I'm coming."

She got out and opened the back of the car. The girls raced out of the SUV in a blur of grey and black. Addie grinned, watching them chase each other through the trees.

Jonah joined her in front of the car. "Whose place is this?"

"Grey's. Well, his family anyway."

"He's from *that* Waverly family?"

She nodded, smiling as the gears turned in his head.

"The rather wealthy agriculture Waverly family?"

"Yeah. Everyone is surprised to learn that. He's pretty down to Earth." She gestured to the house. "This is Harper's place. Grey's older brother."

"He won't mind that we're here?"

She laughed. "No. I'm pretty much an honorary Waverly. Besides, Harper's off in Europe, or somewhere, racing cars."

"Are there other siblings?"

She laughed. "Believe me, two of them are enough." She led the way, meandering through the trees. Lily and Gracey streaked by, tongues lolling from their mouths. "The girls love it here. Plenty of scents to be sniffed, and no need for leashes."

"I love it here." He turned in a small circle before raising his face to the sun. "Nice to be outside."

She smiled, watching him.

"What?" He came closer until he stood next to her, peering down into her face.

"Oh, just you. Despite the injury, I've never seen you so care-free. It's a good look for you."

He palmed her jaw. "Maybe that's because for the first time since I've known you, you aren't being chased by someone intent to kill you." He took another half-step closer. "More likely it's because I'm about to finally kiss you."

That's the only warning she got. Her eyes drifted closed as his lips touched hers. For a moment, the length of a heartbeat, the touch felt like a feather. And then his hand slid into her short curls, binding himself to her. And she was lost.

Addie leaned into the kiss, wanting to press against the length of him. She wrapped one arm around his back, careful not to jostle his injured arm. The kiss went on and on, until both required oxygen.

She broke it and leaned her cheek against his chest. "Well, that was worth the wait."

Laughter rumbled under her ear. "That's putting it mildly." He backed up. Looking into her eyes, Jonah said, "You were worth the wait."

A warmth spread through her chest. "Oh." And then laughed. "I don't know what it is about you that makes me tongue tied."

"Must be my devilish good looks."

"Must be."

"Let's walk." He held his hand out to her, and she placed hers in it. It fit. They fit.

She showed him around the apple orchard. "That's the tree I climbed on a dare from Grey when we were all of six." Rolling up her sleeve, she pointed to a scar. "And that's my reward for falling out of it. But it was all good, once Harper kissed it all better."

He raised that favorite brow of hers. "Harper, huh? Should I be worried?"

She squeezed his hand. "Not at all. I got over that by high school."

"Tell me about your first kiss."

"Danny McCoy, after homecoming sophomore year. They say kissing a smoker is like licking an ash tray." She screwed up her face. "They're right. He and some of the other senior boys snuck out back and smoked cigars and had some drinks. He got a bit fresh with me. Grey came to the rescue."

His expression darkened. "I wish I'd known you back then. I would have rescued you."

She giggled. "I think you've more than made up for lost time."

"Still. He didn't try, uh, anything else, did he?"

"Didn't get the chance." She sighed before continuing. "I was flattered, being asked to the dance by a football player. And a senior at that. Thought I was big stuff. And that would show Tiffany, my arch nemesis."

"You had an arch nemesis in high school? You don't seem like the type."

"What's the type to have one?"

"Oh, I don't know. Maybe a jock or something. Can't picture that."

"Because I trip over my own feet on a regular basis. I get it. I was pretty much a nerd. Always had my nose stuck in a book. And I had Grey. I didn't need anything or anyone else. Anyway, Grey bloomed late, always small for his age. And he was...well, different. So, he started karate early."

"By different, you mean gay."

"Yes. This is a small Southern town. That wasn't an easy thing to be back then. Still isn't sometimes."

"I can imagine."

"Anyway, Grey caught up in high school. Grew a whole foot over our freshman year. Between that and the black belt, no one picked on him. Danny was stupid enough to try something with me. Let's just say that never happened again."

He stopped walking, looked at her for a long moment. Then shook his head. "I didn't know what to make of you two when we first met."

"Most people don't."

"Him acting like an overprotective boyfriend didn't help."

"You got the overprotective part right. Grey would die for me. And me for him."

"Don't say that. You've already come close enough."

"True." She took another few steps before turning to him. "This thing with me and Grey. Is that a problem for you?" She searched his face. "I really hope not. It's a deal breaker."

"I like you, Addie. A lot. And I also like Grey. Even though I wanted to mess him up a bit when we first met."

"You did? Why?"

"Because I thought you were together."

"Ah, how sweet. The Aunties still have to be reminded on a regular basis that Grey and I aren't together."

"Really? Don't they know he's gay?"

"Of course, they do. Just don't choose to believe it. They want babies to cuddle. Before they die." She grimaced. "I hear about that. A lot."

He smothered a grin. "Babies, huh? With Grey?"

"Well, he is my back-up plan. As you know."

"How did Noah feel about that?"

"Is this the part where we discuss our exes?" She didn't want to think about Noah, her last boyfriend. Her up-until-a-few-weeks-ago boyfriend.

"We don't have to."

"Noah didn't like the girls. He also didn't care for Grey. And our closeness. He was doomed from the beginning."

"Not to mention the lack of zing." He leaned in and placed a swift but potent kiss on her lips. "We have zing."

She raised her other hand to her lips, smiling behind it. "We have plenty of zing."

"And I love dogs, especially the girls. And I don't have a problem with Grey. Except for his being your back-up plan. That, I have an issue with."

"I think Jamie probably would as well. They seem to be getting serious. More than three months might be a record for Grey. And besides, that was always theoretical."

"Tell me more about your aunts. They sound, uh, colorful. I've seen them around town in that boat they drive."

"Ah, Betsy. They'd like being described as colorful. Clementine's worst fear is being thought of as a little old lady. Even though that's exactly what she is." Her expression softened. "I'd be lost without them. They're my only family left. Well, other than Grey."

"They raised you, right? After your mom died?"

"Even before that. We, Mom and I, lived with them. Their brother, Thomas, was my grandfather. Mom was their 'miracle', born late in life. He and my grandmother, Susannah, died before I came along. When Mom died, it became the three of us."

"I like them already."

"And they'll love you. Because you can get me pregnant." She tried not to laugh at the look on his face.

"Okay," he replied, dragging two syllables into several.

She doubled over, hugging her sides. When she could finally speak, she pointed to him. "You should see your face, Jonah. My aunts are in their mid-eighties. They want - no, are obsessed with - a baby. And I'm their only option. That's why they loved the idea of Noah. And why they'll love you."

"Not too picky, huh?"

She hit his good arm. "You're a catch by any standards. I'm only telling you to warn you. When they start clucking about babies, you'll know to run for the hills."

"I'm not going anywhere."

The shrieking ghost sound blared from her back pocket. She held up a finger. "Hold that thought." She pulled out her phone. "Hey Grey, what's up?" She stopped walking and listened, unable to get a word in. After a minute, she disconnected.

Jonah looked at her face. "Is something wrong?"

"You could say that." She swallowed hard. "We have to go."

Chapter Four

Addie waited until they were in the car to tell him the bad news. "Something may have happened at the estate sale this morning. And it may have just happened again." She blew her bangs out of her eyes and concentrated on the road ahead of her.

"Start with why we had to leave the farm."

"A man came to the shop, asking for me. I think it may have been the same one I met this morning." Her curled lip showed him what she thought of that.

"What does he want?"

"I bought a box of old books at the sale. They'd been discovered that morning in the cellar. Can you imagine? Leaving poor books to rot in the cellar?"

"The scoundrels!" Jonah's lips quivered. "Sorry. Couldn't resist. You were saying?"

"Fine, I'm a geek about books. Anyway, this man approached me at my car about buying them. I told him no and left. He was rude. Apparently, he didn't take no for an answer and showed up at the shop."

"Hmmm."

She snuck a glance at Jonah. His expression hardened. "I'm sure it's no big deal. Some collectors get a bit, uh, odd."

"Let's hope that's all it is."

She decided against telling him about the dream. For now. Until there came a reason to. They passed the rest of the drive with casual conversation. But tension built in her shoulders as she pulled in behind her bookstore. Things with Jonah were great, and her life had returned to an even keel. Was it too much to ask that they stay that way?

Grey pounced as soon as they walked through the employee entrance. "Young lady, how'd you manage to piss that man off so much?"

"Missed you, too, Grey." She poured some water in a bowl for the girls and pet their heads. Glancing around the shop, she saw that they were free to talk. "Tell me everything."

"He came in and asked for you. I told him you were out and asked how I could help. He said, 'I'm here for the box.' I had no idea what that meant." He cocked his head. "I'm assuming you know what that means."

Addie sighed before settling onto her stool behind the counter. "Let me guess. Early sixties, tweed jacket, English accent?"

"Winner, winner, chicken dinner. Spill."

She filled him in on what she'd already told Jonah. And frowned as Grey's normally sunny expression grew stormy.

"Adelaide Foster! What have I said about not sharing?"

"I know. At the time, it didn't seem like a big deal." *He would freak if he knew about the dream that had prefaced today's events.* She bit her lip. "I'm sorry. I needed it not to mean anything."

Grey came around the counter and enfolded her in his arms. "I know you did. And it still might not be anything huge. No bodies anywhere, after all."

"Funny," muttered Jonah.

"You'll get used to Grey's, uh, humor."

"If you say so."

"Hey. I'm funny."

She patted his arm. "Sure, you are. And I can sing."

"You really can't."

"Exactly."

Jonah held up a hand. "Kids, can we get back to this, please?"

"Of course. What happened after he asked for the box?"

"Before he asked about it, I caught him snooping behind the counter. Or trying to anyway. It got a bit heated. I showed him the door."

She turned to look at the box of books. "I bought it on impulse. Twenty-five for the box. Haven't looked through it yet." She picked up the heavy tome that sat on top and blew a layer of dust off it. Lily gave a dainty sneeze. "Sorry, girl." It bore years of abuse, from the cracked spine to the torn cover. There wouldn't be anything to salvage. She placed it on the counter and opened it. The pages were fragile with age and crackled under her touch. She turned each page, scanning, not knowing what to look for. After the first fifty or so pages, she glanced up. "Something about these books interested him enough to offer me more than I paid for them."

"Not to mention track you down at the store."

"Here we go again," muttered Jonah.

"Maybe it has something to do with the missing treasure," she joked, turning another page.

"Missing treasure? What missing treasure?" inquired Grey.

She kept flipping pages. "Oh, the gentleman at the door today mentioned that Mr. Abernathy had spent his lifetime searching for a buried treasure. 'And never found so much as a doubloon.'"

"Are you kidding me? You didn't think to mention that earlier?" Grey all but vibrated with excitement.

"Don't you have enough money?" Jonah inquired.

"Of course. But I don't have a pirate treasure. How cool would that be?"

"Boys," she muttered, flipping more pages. "Wait a minute. What's this?" She pointed to something written on one of the pages: 34n6m48.2s, 77w58m17.057s.

"Maybe it's code for something. We could break the code and figure out what this means."

"Obviously, you weren't a Boy Scout," snickered Jonah. He pointed to the numbers and letters. "That's GPS positioning of Longitude 34 degrees North, 6 minutes and 48.2 seconds, Latitude of 77 degrees West, 58 minutes, 17.057 seconds. If you put that into your phone's map program, it'll give you a physical location."

"Cool. Let me try." Grey bent over his phone, typing in the information.

"Boy Scout, huh?" Another thing she hadn't known about him, filed away for the future.

"Eagle Scout by the time I finished. Yep, that's me, always prepared."

Grey looked up from his phone. "I may have just thrown up a little in my mouth. But I got the location." She showed his phone to Addie.

She maneuvered the map to get a closer look. "Oh, my goodness." She pointed a fingernail. "I think that's where the Abernathy estate sits."

"And the plot thickens," quipped Grey.

She placed one of her store's bookmarks in the page and continued to flip. By the end, dust floated through the air, but the book held no more information. "I'll go through it again, but that may be all for this one." She glanced down at the other books in the box. "I need to go through those as well."

"It's been a slow day. Why don't you take those home? I'll close up here."

Addie looked around the room. Only one customer stood in her view. "Are you sure?"

"Very. Besides, tomorrow's a big day with all the ankle biters." He shuddered. "You'll want to get your rest before that."

"Should I ask?"

Addie clapped her hands together. "It's only one of my favorite days of the year. Ocean Grove holds its annual Halloween Parade, as you know. Afterwards, the toddler set comes in for a story and snacks."

"Sounds cute," Jonah said.

"'Cute' isn't the first word that comes to mind. It's Addie's deal, not mine. Thank God."

Jonah snorted. "You're afraid of some little kids?"

"Sure, judge me now. Wait and see for yourself."

Addie picked up her purse and whistled for the dogs. "If you two are done, I'm going to take these home and look over them. Hopefully, there's something else of interest stashed away inside one of them."

Jonah straightened away from the counter. "I'm ready."

Grey's eyebrows hit his hairline.

"Oh, okay." She hoped her face wasn't as red as it felt.

"Some unknown guy is trying to find her. Trying to get at these books. We have no idea why or what he's capable of. I'm going with you."

"Sounds like a plan," smirked Grey. "You kids have fun."

"We will," answered Addie, remembering to breathe. He was coming home with her. No big deal. Except it was. A very big deal. *Did she put away her laundry?*

Jonah followed her out to the car. He opened the back door and got the girls settled while she stowed the box on the back seat. Neither spoke until she pulled out onto Magnolia Street.

"Sorry. I should have asked you first." He ran a hand through his longer than she'd ever seen it hair. "I don't like the idea of you being alone in the house after today." He looked over his shoulder to the back of the car. "No offense, girls."

And her heart melted a bit. She took a deep breath. "If you're staying, then we should probably run by your place for, uh, whatever you might need."

"You know where I live."

She took the next right and continued to his townhouse. They'd spent a lot of time together since he'd been shot. But he'd never stayed at her place. Unless you count on the couch that one night when Gwen's killer still roamed the streets of Ocean Grove.

*****

Over an hour later, Addie closed the last of the books, placing it back in the box. "Well, that's disappointing. I really thought we would find something else written in one of these." She kicked the box with her toe.

"At least we eliminated them. Now, we can follow the coordinates from the first book."

"Always this optimistic?" she grumbled.

"More of a realist." Jonah stretched, covering a yawn with his hand. "Sorry. I haven't slept well with this thing." He raised his splint-covered arm.

She hadn't slept well last night either, but she didn't mention that. "That must make things difficult for you. At least the end is within sight."

"It's been a long couple of weeks, that's for sure." He smothered another yawn while sinking a little further into her couch. "I'm not usually this tired."

"My couch has been known to do that to people. It's so comfortable."

"A short nap wouldn't hurt us."

"I had the same thought."

Jonah lifted his good arm, placing it around her shoulders. Addie slid into him, resting her cheek on his chest. "Just a few moments," she murmured.

Addie snuggled into her pillow. Her T-shirt-covered, rock hard pillow. Then realized where she was. A soft chuckle met her ears. She opened her eyes. Shadows filled the room. "I guess we slept a bit longer than a few moments."

"You won't hear me complaining," rumbled in her ear.

A huge smile spread across her face. "As pillows go, you're at the top of my list." She sat up and turned to see him in the dim light.

"Good to know." Jonah sat up as well, leaned in, and covered her lips with his.

And her stomach rumbled.

She broke the kiss, dissolving in laughter on the couch. "I'm so sorry," she eked out.

"No worries. What's for dinner?"

"Grey wasn't kidding. I'm not much of a cook. I am, however, a champion at ordering takeout. And my favorite Italian place delivers. How does that sound?"

He placed a hand over his heart. "Staying in, eating Italian with my girl? Sounds like a plan."

"Great!" She grabbed her phone from the coffee table. "What'll it be?"

"No menus?"

She tapped her temple. "It's all up here. Besides, Giuseppe's has everything you could possibly want."

"How's their Eggplant Parmesan?"

"To die for, pardon the pun."

"Sold!"

She hit a preset and ordered for the two of them. "Forty minutes. That gives me time to feed the dogs and wake up."

"I'm going to use the bathroom."

She started to tell him where it was, but he remembered. He remembered everything about her. She watched him walk away, unsure how she'd gotten so lucky. Smiling to herself, she let the dogs out in the back yard before getting their dinners.

Chapter Five

Jonah's overnight bag sat in her foyer, innocent enough, but it distracted her throughout dinner.

He was staying here tonight. Did her bedroom look like a tornado had hit? Had she shaved?

She swallowed hard and tried to drag her mind back to the conversation. She smiled, hoping he hadn't noticed her mental sidetrack.

He scooped up the last bite of his meal. "Where were you?" he asked before popping it in his mouth.

"Rats!" She felt her face flood with color. "Uh, I mean right here with you." She then placed her fork on the plate and sighed. "Your overnight back is staring at me."

Jonah tilted his head to the side. "Could you say that again? In a way that makes sense to the rest of us?" Then he smiled. "Breathe. It's me. Don't be nervous."

A high-pitched laugh escaped her. "Oh, okay. Why didn't I think of that?"

"There's no pressure. I'm staying here to keep you safe. And because I like spending time with you. Addie, I'm here, with you, because there's nowhere else I'd rather be."

She squeezed his hand before withdrawing hers. "I'll clean this up. Can you let the girls out back for a final walk?"

He did as she asked while she busied herself cleaning up. And breathing. He was here, in her house, and staying the night. She hissed in a breath.

No big deal, Addie. You've had men over before.

But never Jonah. Unless you count the time he slept on the couch with Grey in the guest room. She didn't.

She dried her hands as he brought the girls back in. They dashed to her, wrapping their furry bodies around her legs. It was enough to break the tension. "I just saw you a few minutes ago." She leaned down to hug each of them.

"Are you still freaked out?" Jonah asked from the opposite side of the kitchen. He pushed off from the wall and walked toward her. "I hope not."

"No, of course not." She smiled while her pulse kicked up a bit. "Okay, maybe a little."

"I'm going to take a shower. That gives you a little more time to get used to the idea."

"Let me get you some towels. Everything else you need is in the bathroom." She grabbed some stuff from the linen closet and handed it to him as he passed her with his bag, then watched him walk into her bedroom as if he'd done so a thousand times.

"Well, girls, what do you think of that?" Both dogs tilted their heads but kept their opinions to themselves.

"Not helpful." She sat at the table, stalling, and thought about the dream last night. She gnawed on her lower lip, hoping there wouldn't be a repeat performance tonight.

She shook her head to clear it. "Let's go to bed."

They followed her into the bedroom. Rifling through her drawers, Addie grabbed an old college shirt and a pair of gym shorts. Her normal sleepwear didn't come anywhere near lingerie, but it would do for tonight. She grabbed her phone and dashed off a quick text to Grey.

There's a man in my bathroom. And he's staying. All night.

The bathroom door opened, steam pouring out into the bedroom. He'd put on a pair of running shorts and a faded, navy blue Ocean Grove Police Department T-shirt. Her mouth dried up as she traced the outline of his muscles with her eyes.

He grinned at her. "Do I pass inspection?"

She dropped her gaze. "Sorry. Uh, let me grab an extra pillow for your arm."

He reached out with his good hand to grab her wrist. "Addie, relax. It's me."

She looked at him, dressed informally, and giggled. "You don't look like a detective at the moment."

"Well, I'm not wearing my gun, if that's what you mean."

"I'm being ridiculous. Sorry."

"Relax. We both need our sleep." He frowned at his splint. "And this thing doesn't exactly lend itself to romance."

She blew out a breath, fluffing her bangs out of her eyes. "Okay." She smiled, a real one that reached her eyes. "You still need a pillow for that arm. I'm not sharing mine. I like a lot of pillows. Be right back."

She walked out of the bedroom to the hallway linen closet. After grabbing a spare pillow, she made the rounds to make sure all the windows and doors were locked. Satisfied, she set the alarm and returned to her bedroom.

"Are we all tucked in?" He laughed at the expression on her face. "I heard you set the alarm. Good girl."

Addie tossed the pillow on the bed. Then walked right up to Jonah and kissed him. A good, solid kiss. "There. I feel better with that out of the way. Calmer. Okay, let's get you situated."

He frowned. "I'm not an eighty-year-old woman."

"I know."

"Good. Just checking."

"Men! Now get into bed." She stood next to his side of the bed while he got in. After he got situated, she placed the pillow under his left arm. "I'll only be a minute."

She walked into the bathroom and rushed through her night-time routine. After washing her face, she glanced at her expression. And grinned. Jonah was in her bed. She patted her face dry and left the bathroom.

"Light on or off?"

"Whatever you prefer."

"Off, then." She switched off the light and climbed into her side of the bed. And lay on her back with eyes wide open. Not the least bit tired, despite the long day.

*****

The next morning, Addie rushed around, trying not to be late for work. Having Jonah here, while lovely, slowed her down. Distracted her. In the best possible way. They'd lingered over breakfast until she ran out of time. She dropped him off at home and headed to work. Then remembered she'd forgotten her purse.

Cursing under her breath, she headed back home. She left the car running and ran up to the front door. And stopped in her tracks. A huge bouquet of flowers sat on her welcome mat. Very formal flowers that made her think of a funeral. A little too large. A little too perfect. Her smile drooped. Surely, Jonah knew her better than this. She plucked the card from it. 'Thinking of you.' Pushing the flowers aside, she ran in and grabbed her purse. After resetting the alarm, she locked the door and picked up the flowers. She'd deal with them at work.

She arrived before Grey, giving herself time to ensure the store was ready for the Halloween party. Not sure what to do with the flowers, but not wanting to be rude, she placed them on a low table in the sitting area. She wandered around the shop, straightening and ensuring everything looked perfect. Her mind kept returning to the strange Englishman and numbers written in that book.

"Must we be invaded by ankle biters?" Grey said by way of hello.

He didn't share her beliefs on the matter. "You don't have to stay. I know how you feel about all this. Might I remind you that the 'ankle biters' come with parents? Parents who buy books. Which, in turn, keeps this place going." She frowned at him. "Not that you need the money."

"Even if I wasn't insanely rich, I wouldn't mess with those little hooligans." He spied the vase of flowers and screwed up his face. "What is that?"

"I'm guessing you didn't send them, then."

"What? Why? I love you. I'd never send those. Even if you were dead."

"What?"

"They look like something one would send to a funeral. Someone else. I wouldn't. They're hideous." He snickered. "Do not tell me Detective Hottie sent those! That's a definite strike one."

"Huh, that's what I thought. The part about the funeral. The card didn't have a name."

"That's odd."

"Another mystery." She glanced at her phone. "Well then, you have about five minutes before they 'invade'. Which means I have five minutes to get into my costume. Be right back."

Addie ran to her office and locked the door behind her. Every year, she dressed as a character from a children's book for this event. This year, she would be Cindy Lou Who from Dr. Seuss's *The Grinch That Stole Christmas*. She donned a pink nightgown that brushed her toes. That was the easy part. The blonde wig not so much. She wrestled her own dark hair up under it and then turned to the mirror hanging on the back of her office door. Her blonde reflection made her giggle. She shrugged and attached two red ribbons in the wig. Two large spots of blusher on her cheeks completed the look. Satisfied she'd done the best she could, she left her office.

And ran right into Jonah.

He braced her with his good hand. "Whoa."

"Sorry. The last thing you need is me running you over."

He smiled and pointed to his splint. "Even with this, I think I can handle you." His eyes drifted from her now blonde hair to her toes. "Interesting look. For what's it worth, I prefer your normal hair color."

She'd never need that added blush at this rate. "Thank you, kind sir. I am Cindy Lou Who, in case you didn't know."

"'Who was no more than two'?"

"Exactly. It's for the Halloween party that's about to happen. Aren't you early?"

"No. I'm right on time." He glanced down at his khakis and sweatshirt. "I didn't dress up for the party, but I thought I could help."

And just like the Grinch, her heart grew three sizes. "You didn't have to do that." She leaned up and kissed his cheek. "But I'm glad you did. Follow me."

She led him to the children's section and pointed to a low table in the corner. "I have to put out the cookies and juice boxes. You can help Grey with that. He'll be ducking out as soon as everything is set up. Not a fan of kids."

"I love kids. I have several nieces and nephews. Not that that fact stops my mom from grilling me about giving her more grandkids."

"Thanks. I always greet the children as they come in." She cocked her head as the bell over the door chimed. "And here they come." She hurried off to greet her first arrival.

Within fifteen minutes, she'd welcomed princesses, cowboys, a few Star Wars characters, several superheroes, and one adorable newborn dressed as peas in a pod. When the children sat on the carpet, she took her place on a chair in front. She tried to ignore the fact that Jonah watched her every move. Tried.

"Wow, you guys look great! Thank you all for coming today. Before I read our first book, can anyone guess who I'm dressed as?"

A few little hands waved in the air. She pointed to a little boy, maybe four years old, dressed as a scarecrow. "Who do you think?"

He stood up, then looked to his mother, who nodded and smiled. "Are you that little girl from The Grinch?"

Addie clapped her hands. "I am. Good guess, Mr. Scarecrow." The little boy's face glowed with pride. "Can you tell me the name of that character?"

His smile wavered a bit. "Cindy Sue?"

Several of the kids laughed, and his smile turned into a frown.

"Oh, my goodness, you were so close. It's Cindy Lou. Now come up here and pick a prize." She held up a plastic pumpkin with dollar store choices in it.

The scarecrow came up to her and plunged his tiny hand into the pumpkin. He pulled out a black spider ring. "Cool!" He placed it on his finger and made his way back to his seat. After a nod from his mother, he yelled, "Thank you."

"You're more than welcome. Now, let's start with *Skeleton Hiccups*, by Margery Cuyler."

She read the book aloud while the children giggled at the antics of the skeleton and his ghost friend trying to cure his hiccups. She never got tired of that sound. When she finished, a lively discussion began on how to best cure the hiccups. One small girl dressed as a pumpkin demonstrated by standing on her head.

She read one more book before inviting the children to the treat table. Several parents approached her about purchasing the books she'd read to the kids. Others thanked her for hosting the event. Several of the moms attended her monthly women's book club. Other than the sheer joy of being surrounded by books, this was her favorite part.

"Nicely done," he whispered just above her right ear.

Addie turned, smiling up at him. "This is so much fun for me. If I can share my joy of reading with just one of these little ones, my job here is done."

"I think it's safe to say you've accomplished that."

She glanced across the sea of costume clad cuties. "You may be right. I've known some of these guys since they were babies. That's one of the many things I love about living in Ocean Grove. Getting to know people and watching their families grow. Many of them start out as customers and end up becoming good friends."

She peeked at Grey, manning the register. Out of the reach of small, sticky hands. Quite a few people waiting to purchase books. She performed a mental happy dance.

"Today is a win-win. Kids have a good time, and I sell books. What else could I ask for?" She glanced at the wall clock. "Erin should be here any second. I'm going to change, then we can get going."

"I can help Grey clean up while you change."

"Thanks, Jonah."

She went back to her office and closed the door. After removing the blush from her face, she took off the wig and shook out her short curls. She took off the nightgown, folded it, and put it in a bag. Then she pulled on capris and an old UNCW sweatshirt. Years of wear and tear had taken their toll, fading the color and leaving the cuffs ragged. That's what made it her favorite.

She came out and looked around. She spotted Grey in the children's section. Safe now that they were all gone. And Jonah stood in the sitting area. Staring at the flowers he'd sent her. She approached him.

He pointed at the huge arrangement. "You didn't mention these."

"Oh, I forgot, what with all the hullabaloo here. Thank you so much." She leaned in and kissed him quickly on the mouth before heading behind the counter. She stopped to pat Gracey and Lily on their silky heads. "Next year, girls, I really ought to dress y'all up for Halloween." Both dogs grinned and wagged their tails.

"For what?"

She turned to Jonah. "Huh?"

"You thanked me, but I'm not sure what for. Although I'll take another kiss anytime."

"Eww, not again. Do I have to break out my cat coughing up a hairball noise? What is it with you two?"

She and Grey looked from the flowers to each other to him. "I, uh, thought they were from you. The card wasn't signed, but I...oh." She felt her cheeks burn and ducked her head.

"You thought I sent *those*?" He shook his head. "We may not know each other very well, but I'd like to think I know you better than that. Those belong at a funeral."

"A ha! That's what I said."

"Grey, shush."

"But I was right."

She sighed. "Fine, you were right." She turned back to the flowers, which she now liked even less. "I didn't know. It's not like there's a line of guys waiting to send me flowers."

"Well, there's at least two. And for the record, I would bring you something less formal, maybe wildflowers."

"Oh." She grinned. "Those are my favorite."

"Lucky guess," Grey muttered.

"No, not lucky. These are too perfect. They're symmetrical, for God's sake."

"That's what I said."

"And then there's the color. Or lack thereof. Only red, pink, and white?" He shook his head. "Addie is all about the chaos. She wants all the colors. And it works for her."

"I do want all the colors. And I love wildflowers."

"There's time for flowers. There's time for a lot of things, Addie."

She gazed deep into his chocolate brown eyes. "Yes, there is."

"Well, if you didn't send them, who did?"

Jonah's eyes hardened until they were almost black. "That's what I want to know."

Chapter Six

A chill snaked down Addie's back, despite the warmth of the store. She pointed to the card. "I didn't notice before, but there isn't a florist's name on this. Not that I get a lot of flowers, but doesn't the card usually have the florist's name?"

Jonah leaned in to read the card. "You're right. And the note doesn't thrill me either. 'Thinking of you'? Who's thinking of you?"

Grey straightened from his casual pose against the desk. "Good question."

She rubbed her hands up and down her arms. "I don't like this. Not one bit. I didn't like them from the moment I found them on my porch this morning, but I thought they were f rom you."

One ebony brow raised. "You found them on your porch? I assumed they came to the store."

"I ran home to grab my purse after dropping you off. They sat on the welcome mat."

"Not very welcoming," said Grey with a smirk.

Jonah fixed him with a glare. "There's nothing funny about this."

The smirk slid from Grey's handsome face. "No, of course not. Sorry, Addie."

"No worries." She turned to Jonah. "That's his version of my verbal diarrhea when I get nervous. He gets snippier."

"You mean funnier or more sarcastic."

"If that helps you sleep at night."

Jonah held up his good hand. "Before that deteriorates any further, can we get back to the issue at hand? Someone, some man I presume, sent these to Addie. Someone who's 'thinking of her'."

"When you put it that way." She shuddered.

Jonah walked around the corner of the counter. He stopped next to her, hugging him to her with his good arm. "I'm not about to let anything happen to you, Addie."

The fervor behind his words lifted the chill a bit. "I know you won't. And we really don't know what they mean, if anything." She may have added that last part to comfort herself.

"We don't, but I think you can't be too careful. Especially since they were delivered by hand to your door. Whoever sent them knows where you live."

And the chill returned. "What do we do?"

"And she's off," uttered Grey.

Jonah shook his head. "*We* don't do anything. *I* will make some calls. Can I borrow your office?"

"Of course, but I can make calls."

He headed in that direction.

Grey leaned across the counter and squeezed her hand. "Let him do this, Addie. It's a guy thing."

"It is?"

"It is. You've seen him injured and unconscious. He feels like he needs to make up for that. It's like the time Jamie saw my unfortunate display when I spotted a spider in the kitchen." He shuddered as if remembering.

"I hardly think those are the same things. Jonah could have died. The worst that could have happened to you was fall off the chair."

"Give the lady a Kewpie doll. Exactly my point. You saw him at his worst. And all those times you drove him to PT and the doctor? That's got to be tough for a big, strong, handsome detective to take."

Her face fell. "Oh. I never thought of it like that. I probably should have let him take the garbage out last night."

"Yep."

She sat on the stool and cupped her chin in her hand. "This relationship thing is hard."

"Tell me about it."

"I've been alone for a long time. I haven't had to think about this stuff." She blew the curls out of her eyes.

"True. There hasn't been anyone in a while. Well, except Noah." His mouth formed a perfect O. "You don't think Noah sent them, do you?"

"No. He didn't care that much about me. We'd only been on about five dates."

"But he didn't care for you breaking up with him in public. Maybe for breaking up with him at all."

She shook her head. "I really don't see him doing this. I haven't even heard from him."

"Heard from who?"

They both startled at the question. "Grey asked if I thought Noah could have sent them."

Jonah's mouth flattened into a hard line. "And you don't?"

She thought about that for a second.

"Addie?"

"I don't think he did. It seems more emotional, for lack of a better word, than anything he ever did when we dated."

Grey shook his head.

"What? Spit it out."

"Addie always thought I made it up. But I didn't. He looked at her funny. When he thought she didn't see."

"Looked at her? How?"

"Like he could picture the whole thing: white picket fence, kids in the yard. And they hadn't even, you know."

"Grey! That has nothing to do with anything." She turned to Jonah, trying to ignore her hot cheeks. "Grey is a slut."

"True."

"He thinks it was such a big deal that we'd had five dates without having sex." She stopped for a second and thought about that. "Without doing much of anything, really. Hmmm."

"I'm glad to hear it. Not the picket fence part."

"Oh."

He smiled at her. "You say that a lot around me."

"You make me speechless a lot."

"That's saying something. Noah never left her speechless."

"Good. Let me make another call." He started to turn away.

"Please don't get Noah in trouble. I doubt he did this."

"You can't be sure, and I need to be. I'll be discreet." He took his phone from his back pocket and dialed. "Dan, I have something else for you," he said before moving out of earshot.

She shook her head and turned to Grey. "Will there ever be a time when Jonah and I can just be Jonah and I?"

"Oh, sweetie." He leaned down and kissed her head. "At least he doesn't think you're a suspect this time."

She swatted him on the shoulder. "Nice." He had a point, though she wouldn't be sharing that with him.

"You know what I mean. He's always going to be a detective. And you're always going to be you."

"And by that, you mean...?"

"So sensitive today. All I'm saying is that this is the third time, since July, that you've gotten into something."

"All I did was get random flowers."

"From an unknown guy. Let's not forget the professor who wants your estate sale purchase. At any cost."

"Oh. That."

"Are we ready to go treasure hunting?" Jonah asked as he rejoined them.

"Just waiting on Erin. What did you find out?"

"Nothing yet."

"But you asked someone named Dan about the flowers, didn't you?"

"She has the ears of an, hmmm, well, whatever has really good hearing."

Jonah laughed. "I'll have to remember that. I did ask Dan, a fellow detective, to make a few calls. And before you protest, I did it to feel better about the flowers."

"I wasn't going to protest," she muttered. "Okay, maybe. Doesn't he have more important things to do?"

"Nothing more important than keeping you safe."

"Oh."

"I love it when you shut her up like that. It's so rare."

"You shut it, Grey, or you can stay home." She laughed as his face fell, making him look like a pouting toddler.

"But I want to go. I even have a shovel."

"What? Why?" Jonah asked.

"Because he thinks we're going to find buried treasure today." She stuck out her tongue at Grey. "You really think we're going to go out there and find buried treasure? On the first attempt? Mr. Abernathy spent a lifetime pursuing this without any success."

"But what if we do? Huh? Did you think of that?"

"He has a point. That would be cool," Jonah agreed.

She whirled on him, hands on hips. "Not you, too."

He smirked. "I love it when she gets all feisty. Of course, we're not going to find anything today."

Grey's smile turned into a frown. "But we could."

"Sure. And aliens could walk through the door."

The bell over the door tinkled, and three heads whipped in that direction. And in walked an alien. Or Erin dressed as one.

Addie doubled over laughing.

Jonah stared.

Grey raised a fist in the air. "Yes!"

"Erin dressed as an alien doesn't count."

The alien in question walked around the counter, placing her purse under it. "What?"

Jonah looked at Addie, still gasping for air around her laughter. "It's a long story. Nice costume."

Grey ran up to her and kissed her cheek. "Welcome, my little good luck charm."

"Really, guys, what?"

Addie wiped her hands under her eyes. "You had to be there. But I'm glad to see you. Sure you're okay with watching the store yourself?"

"The ankle biters are all gone. You should be good," added Grey.

"Aw, I would have liked to see them." She turned to Addie. "Were they adorable? I bet they were. Especially the tiny ones in their fuzzy costumes."

Grey motioned with his head towards the door to Jonah. "Hurry, before we grow an ovary."

"I like kids. Wouldn't mind having a couple myself." His eyes sought Addie's.

A huge smile lit her face as warmth grew in her belly. "Me either."

"Oh. My. God. I can practically hear your biological clock ticking. Both of you."

"Don't worry, Uncle Grey, I won't ask you to babysit." She whistled at the girls. They both jumped off the bed they shared behind the counter, all wagging tails and lolling tongues. "Who wants to go for a ride in the country?" That set off a chorus of excited yips.

She fastened their leashes and grabbed her purse. "Thanks again, Erin, for coming in."

"No problem. I have a party on campus later, in case you hadn't guessed."

"Well, have fun with that. And be careful." She thought of her assistant like a younger sister and didn't want anything to happen to her.

"The party is on campus, and I'll be walking to it. I'll be fine."

"Yes, Mama Bear, she'll be fine. Maybe you should have your own baby." He grinned. "Or we could still have that baby we've always talked about."

That brought a dark scowl from Jonah, as Addie knew Grey had intended.

"Keep it up, and we'll leave you here." She headed out, with the girls prancing in front of her.

Jonah held the door for her. Grey brought up the rear, laughing all the way.

"I know you two go way back and all. But he really has to stop mentioning that in front of me."

Addie patted his arm before opening the back hatch of her SUV. "Our agreement to have a child together was only in good fun. And if we were both single at forty. Neither of us is single anymore. And nowhere near forty."

Closer than she would like, but not that close yet.

Jonah leaned in until only she could hear. "I like that you know you're off the market." He gave her a swift but powerful kiss and headed to the front passenger seat.

She pressed one hand to her mouth, enjoying the electricity coursing through her body. Her lips tingled.

"Sometime today," yelled Grey, relegated to the back seat.

"Okay, I'm coming. Don't get your panties in a twist." She slid into the driver's seat. "Let's go find some buried treasure."

Chapter Seven

Being the driver has its perks, Addie thought as she picked a satellite radio station dedicated to Tom Petty. "That's enough out of you two," she gloated. For the past twenty minutes, the two men had bickered, there really wasn't any other word for their behavior, over music to play in the car. She tapped her fingers on the wheel to the tune of "American Girl".

A disgruntled snort came from the back seat. She ignored it.

"Petty, huh? Never would have guessed that," remarked Jonah from the passenger seat.

"Oh?" She stole a look at his face. "And what would you have guessed?"

"Not sure, but not classic rock. Maybe nineties stuff?"

Grey leaned up between the seats. "Is that sweat on your forehead?"

"Play nice. You have the advantage of knowing me since we were single digits."

"Are you going to tell me if I was right?"

"Yes and no. I like some of that. I love Pearl Jam and some of Nirvana's stuff. Never got into the whole grunge scene though. I have eclectic taste when it comes to music."

"And a lot of things. Except men, of course," added Grey.

"That's enough out of the peanut gallery. I meant art, movies, books, food. Things like that."

"And men? Not so much?"

"She's always had a thing for DBMs. Haven't you, Addie?"

Her hands tightened on the steering wheel. Addie looked straight ahead, trying to ignore the fact that her face flamed.

"Should I ask?"

"No," she replied.

"Of course," Grey replied.

She let out a sigh and loosened her grip. No use breaking a nail over this. "Dark. Brooding. Male."

"Oh."

Laughter roared from the back seat.

"Ignore him. I do."

"And yet I'm still your BFF."

"Some days," she gritted out.

"Do you find me brooding?"

She turned her head for a minute to steal a glance. "Not at the moment." She turned her attention back to the road.

"When did I brood?"

Another round of laughter exploded from the back. "You're kidding, right?"

"Brooding? I don't brood. I think. I solve things. I am a detective."

She glanced again, wishing she could smooth the line of his jaw. "They go together, the dark and brooding. Until very recently, you always acted seriously around me."

"That's called professionalism. Your life was in danger."

"Yes, all true. But that didn't stop me from wanting to kiss your dimple. Or run my hands through your hair to see if it felt as soft as I hoped."

"Oh. Maybe DBM isn't such a bad thing after all."

"Gag."

"Shut up, Grey," they both said at the same time.

"See, you're learning."

He grinned at her. "I am. I wouldn't classify Noah as a DBM."

"Exactly," called Grey. "Now you're getting it, Heathcliff."

Addie tuned on her blinker. "Oh look, we're here." *Thank goodness.* She drove down the lane leading up to the estate. The place looked deserted. "Where should I park?"

Jonah looked at his phone. "The coordinates lead into the woods. Wherever you want, I guess."

She drove the rest of the way to the house, then around to the right, pulling in under a car port in the back. Addie walked around to the back and let out the girls. She clipped the twelve-foot leashes she kept in the car to their collars.

"Okay, lead the way." She hit the lock button on her key fob and then slid the keys into her pocket.

Jonah handed Grey his phone. "You might be better doing this, since you have two hands. And you won't need that shovel."

"Fine." He tucked the shovel in question under his arm and looked at the screen. "Not very far. Maybe a half-mile into the woods. Can you keep up?"

"I broke my arm, not my leg. I'll be fine."

"Should have just brought you guys," she muttered to the girls. Then smiled at their antics. Both had their noses in the air and tails up. Must be plenty of things to sniff. She started off across the pavement to the edge of the woods.

"Coming alone wouldn't have been your best plan. Even if Grey is being a pain. You have to make safe choices, Addie." He reached down and grabbed her hand, giving it a squeeze.

She snorted. "I'm really afraid of a guy in his early sixties."

"Who may or may not have been carrying a gun."

"Not to mention your secret admirer," added Grey, catching up with them.

"Gee, thanks for reminding me."

"I haven't forgotten," added Jonah in a dark tone.

"And the DBM is back, lady and gentleman." He smirked at 'the look' from Addie. "You know that's never worked on me." But he shut up and followed along.

Addie fell in step with Jonah, holding his hand and the leashes in her other. The girls pranced out to the end of their leashes, sniffing every leaf and twig they found. The warmth of his hand delighted her. She'd been alone a long time. Noah didn't really count. They'd only been on five dates. And he never held her hand like this. She smiled up at Jonah.

He smiled back, looking less fierce. "You look happy."

She squeezed his hand and kept walking.

He squeezed back.

They walked along in a comfortable silence. Unless you counted Grey's endless chatter. Addie didn't. After almost thirty years of friendship, it became white noise to her. Until the pitch of his voice rose. Like it just did. Then she listened.

"This is it." He stood on the spot given in the coordinates and looked all around him. His shoulders dropped. "I was so sure."

"Of what? That there would be a treasure chest waiting? Or a sign with an arrow that read 'Dig here'?" Jonah didn't bother to hide his snicker.

Addie sat on a fallen tree to tie her sneaker. "If it was that easy, Grey, Mr. Abernathy would have found it years ago."

He pulled a can of red spray paint from his backpack and placed a large dot on the trunk of the tree.

"Wouldn't an X be a better choice?" asked Jonah, tongue firmly in cheek.

"It would be the obvious one. We can't have that. Someone else might find it."

"Find what, exactly?"

"The first clue to the buried treasure, of course." His tone was one Addie used when talking with toddlers.

Jonah didn't seem to mind. "Oh. You're expecting more clues?"

"Well, of course. How else would we find the buried treasure?"

"And where will we find these clues?"

Grey's smile dimmed. "Well, that I don't know. Yet..." He turned to her. "Addie, you must have a plan. You love a good mystery."

She rose from her seat on the log. "Yes, I do. But I don't know where to start with this one. Jonah and I searched the other books. Nothing."

"Okay." He paced around the tree. "How about other books at the sale?"

Addie laughed. "You wouldn't believe how many books that library contained. Thousands. It would take forever to check each one."

"Plus, the sale ended, and this is private property. We can't just waltz in there."

"Ever the practical one," groused her BFF.

"Well, I am a cop."

"Jonah's right." She looked around the woods, the hairs on her neck rising. "We really shouldn't even be here. Let's go. We can brainstorm in the car."

They trooped back to the car. Addie almost bit a hole in her tongue trying not to laugh at Grey. He'd been so sure they'd find something. She focused on the girls instead, running here and there to the ends of their leashes. Her life should be that easy.

They piled back in her car. She sat for a moment, looking up at the imposing stone manor home. "Can you imagine the secrets those walls hold?"

"If only they can tell us the location of the buried treasure," groused Grey from the back seat.

"What fun would that be?" She smiled at him in the rear-view mirror before starting the car. "Too easy."

They discussed various plans to hunt for the fortune all the way back to the store. She slammed on the brakes as a small black car barreled out of the side street, next to her store, barely missing them.

"What the..." She hit the horn, but the car had vanished. Addie pulled into her parking space in the back. Her phone rang, Erin's smiling face showing up on the screen. She swiped across to answer.

"I'm back," she attempted to tell her, but Erin's sobbing broke through.

"Addie, hurry. Please. This horrible man scared me."

Grey shot out of the back seat, running for the door.

Jonah turned to her. "I'll get the girls. Go!"

She took off after Grey. By the time she reached the counter inside, panting a bit too much for her comfort, she found Erin sobbing in Grey's arms. She approached them, rubbing the girl's back. "What happened?"

Erin let go of Grey, and Addie led her to the grouping of chairs in the corner. "Sit down and collect yourself. Grey, get her some water."

She sat in the chair next to Erin. "Okay, deep breath. Tell me what happened."

Erin gave a weak smile through her tears. "I hope I'm not overreacting. But he frightened me."

"Who did?"

"The man who came in asking me about some books you bought at that sale yesterday."

The tiny hairs on the back of her neck stood at attention. "You're not overreacting, Erin. If he scared you, you have the right to be upset." She took one of her cold hands in her own, rubbing it. "Now, start from the beginning."

Erin took a deep, shuddery breath and let it out slowly. "I saw him come in, maybe ten minutes ago. I stood at the counter, ringing up some customers. You know how you always look up when the bell rings over the door?"

Addie nodded. "I do. What did he do when he came in?"

"He looked at me, then walked further into the store. I didn't give it a thought, since I was ringing up customers. And then he approached the desk."

"He waited until you were done with others? Until you were alone?"

Her slender frame shook. "I didn't think of it like that, but yeah. We were alone in the store at that point."

Addie's mouth flattened into a hard line. *How dare he scare this young girl like that?*

Grey walked over, sitting in the chair on the other side of Erin. He handed her a bottled water. "What did I miss?"

"Not much. Erin was just telling me how our mystery man waited until they were alone in the store to approach her." She hid a smile watching his hands curl into fists in his lap. Grey took care of his own.

"Did he?"

Jonah walked in, led by two happy Shelties. The girls rushed Erin. She buried her face in their thick fur and sobbed. He stopped in his tracks, wringing the leashes in his hands. She'd have laughed at his obvious discomfort if the situation wasn't dire.

Addie looked up when another man walked in the door.

Jonah nodded. "Thanks for coming."

The man grinned and headed straight for her, hand extended. "You must be the famous Adelaide."

She laughed, shaking his hand. "Not sure about famous, but please call me Addie."

"I'm Dan Blackwell. Nice to officially meet you." He held her hand a bit too long. Until Jonah growled in his direction.

Chapter Eight

"Hands off, Dan." Jonah smiled as he said it, but Addie felt the tension radiating between the two men.

The detective grinned and let go. "That's how it is, huh?"

Addie slid up to Jonah, hooking her arm around his waist. "Yep, that's how it is." She turned towards the chairs. "Come meet Erin. She just told us what happened."

She introduced Dan to everyone. They all took a seat. "Erin, can you tell Detective Blackwell what you just told me?"

The younger woman raised red-rimmed eyes to him. "Sure."

"Please, call me Dan."

Addie hoped his jovial manner was meant to put Erin at ease. Still, it rubbed her the wrong way. And if she hadn't glanced at Jonah, she would have missed the subtle tightening in his jaw.

Erin told the beginning over again. "This will sound odd, but his smile sent chills down my spine. I'd been busy helping customers. And he appeared out of nowhere, with this smile that seemed off. He got right to the point, didn't waste time chatting. He asked for you, Addie, by name. Not just 'Is the owner here?'"

Her stomach tightened at that, but she kept a smile on her face for Erin. "Go on."

"He said something like, 'All I want is the box of books. Be a good girl and get them for me.' I told him I only work here part-time. That I didn't know what he meant." She sat back in her chair and gulped. "He didn't like my answer. He never raised his voice, but his tone told you how angry he was. He said, 'Don't play dumb, little girl. Things could get ugly.'" She broke off on a sob.

"You're doing great, Erin. Anything else?" She rubbed her arm.

"I backed away from the counter. He kept leaning in, you know, crowding me. His eyes were flat, dead. He started to come around the counter when the bell rang over the door. He turned towards it. A family walked in, including a father who was big. I think that scared him. He turned back to me and whispered, 'You tell Ms. Foster this isn't over. Not by a long shot.' Then he left. And I called you. I don't know what would have happened if that family hadn't come in just then."

She didn't either. "I'm sorry, Erin. He never should have approached you like that. I'll make sure you're not alone in the store again."

Erin gave a wan smile. "I'd appreciate that." She shook her head. "He looked so mild when he walked in. Who's afraid of an older man wearing elbow patches?" She eked out a high laugh. "I guess that saying about judging books by their covers is right."

Dan leaned forward in his chair. "Good job, Erin." He turned to Addie. "Jonah tells me you know this guy."

"I don't know his name." She told him about the estate sale. Grey added the man's first visit to the store.

The detective nodded, then wrote some notes. He asked about cameras in and around the store.

"We have them everywhere. I can get you the tapes."

"Good." He rose and turned to Jonah. "I'll be in touch."

Addie rose as well. "That's all?"

He smiled at her in that way she started to hate. "What else is there to do? We have a general description of a man. He didn't put his hands on her. His threat was weak at best. And unspecific."

"Wait. You're telling me he has to hurt someone before you can do anything about it?"

"What I'm saying is that I'll look at the tapes, see if I can identify him. It's the best I can do."

She counted to ten in her head. "Well, thank you for that." She'd already dismissed him. Smiling Detective Dan wasn't going to help. Luckily, she knew another, better detective.

"I'll see myself out. Jonah, enjoy the rest of your vacation."

He answered with a nod of his head and steely glint in his eye. "Sure thing."

Addie waited until he left the store before exploding. "Well, that makes me feel better. Not." She turned to Erin. "Why don't you go home? Try to enjoy your party tonight." She winced at the green face paint that had been smudged by her tears.

"Thanks, Addie. I think I will." She walked to the counter to grab her stuff, then left the store with a small wave of her hand.

"Before you say anything, Dan is the only other detective we have. Ocean Grove isn't Atlanta." He sighed. "He isn't exactly energetic at his job."

"You think? I just met him and could tell you that," Grey muttered. "Too bad you're still 'on vacation.'"

"No matter. On leave doesn't stop me from helping."

"That's the best thing I've heard all afternoon. Tell me how we can help."

"Again with the 'we'?" Jonah groaned.

"Have you not met her? You might as well go with it. She's a pit bull."

"Don't remind me."

"Still in the room, boys. I'm not suggesting a stake-out or anything. But there must be something I can do to help."

"Give her a task, Jonah. She'll come up with one on her own if you don't."

"You can be fired at any time, Grey."

He swooped Addie up in his arms, spinning her around before setting her back down. "True, but you can't fire me as your BFF."

"You got me." She leaned up and kissed his cheek. "Now, out you go. Have fun with Jamie tonight."

He winked at her. "We will. That five-hundred-dollar prize for best costume is as good as ours. See you." He left through the back door.

"Alone at last."

She turned to him with a smile. "Soon. Let me pick up a bit." She glanced at her phone. "I'm going to close a little early. Then we can grab takeout and eat at my house." She blew him a kiss. "I'll even let you pick."

"Sounds like a plan. And we can stop at my place on the way. I need more clothing." He grinned. "I'll be staying the night. For your protection, of course."

A delicious flutter sailed through her belly. She met his gaze as a wicked grin materialized on her mouth. "Of course. But who's going to protect you?"

*****

The aroma of Mexican food tickled Addie's nose as she pulled into her driveway more than an hour later. "I don't know about you but figuring out this mystery makes me hungry."

Jonah smiled as he exited her SUV. "What doesn't make you hungry?" he joked. Walking to the back of the car, he lifted the hatch, releasing the girls. They raced to the grass and squatted, then chased each other to the front porch.

"I'd call you on that. But we both know it's true." She grabbed the takeout bag and her purse before locking the doors and heading to the porch.

"It's a good thing there's been so many mysteries lately. You would have wasted away to nothing if not." He grabbed her around the waist with his good arm and placed a quick kiss on her mouth. "Can't have that happening. I've gotten used to you being around."

She unlocked the front door and dashed inside to silence the alarm. "Nice save," she tossed over her shoulder.

"All true."

Warmth spread throughout her chest. "Come on in. Make yourself comfortable. I'm going to feed the girls first, then we can eat. You know how they can be. You'll have one of them, Gracey probably, right in your face if I don't."

She whistled for them and walked into the kitchen. After serving up their dinner, she rejoined him in the living room. "Okay, our turn."

"Our dinner has been teasing me all the way here." Jonah's stomach rumbled, underlining his words. "You're not the only one who likes to eat."

"Is the kitchen table okay?"

"Anywhere works." He held up his good hand. "I got tacos to make eating easier."

"Good thinking. I thought maybe you celebrated Taco Tuesday early."

He tilted his head and grinned. "I could get behind Taco Sunday. Taco any day of the week, really."

She grinned back at him. "I knew I liked you for a reason." She turned, leading the way back into the kitchen.

"Maybe, over dinner, you could tell me some of those reasons."

"Maybe." She grabbed drinks while Jonah made himself comfortable at her table.

"Ah, playing hard to get. I like a challenge."

"Good. Then you can help me figure out this buried treasure thing."

"Grey wasn't joking. You become a pit bull."

She stuck out her tongue. "Only when I have to. That man threatened Erin. It doesn't matter that your detective friend didn't take it seriously." She dropped into her chair, gut churning at the thought of some stranger frightening Erin.

Jonah covered her hand with his. "I take it very seriously."

"Thank you. Erin deserves better than that."

"Yes, she does. So, do you. We'll figure this out."

Addie turned her hand over to squeeze his before pulling it back. "Right now, it's taco time." She handed two beef tacos to Jonah and placed her own fish tacos on her plate.

Only the sound of chewing and occasional whine from an interested Sheltie broke the silence as they devoured their food. Addie finally came up for air. "Wow! Those are amazing." She wiped her mouth on a paper towel. "Can we talk about you-know-what now?"

"You mean the average velocity of an unladen swallow?" Jonah popped the last bite of his taco into his mouth, chewing with a bit of a smirk.

She knew her mouth hung open but couldn't do anything about it. "You just quoted Monty Python to me. I might be a little in love with you."

The smirk became a grin. "Only a little?"

Her pulse beat wildly in her throat. "That all depends. Can you quote *Life of Brian* as well?"

He held her gaze. "Blessed are the cheesemakers."

She laid a hand over her chest. "Be still my heart."

"About this other thing. There are really two things we need to look at. First, who is our English friend? Second, what else can we discover about the alleged buried treasure?"

"Grey would faint if he heard you doubt the existence of the buried treasure. I've been thinking. What if I can get back into the estate? Maybe look around the basement." She burst out laughing at the look on his face. "With permission, of course."

"Whew. For a moment, I thought you were suggesting breaking and entering. Again."

"We didn't break last time." She dropped her eyes to the table. "Just entered."

"And almost got yourself and Grey killed."

"In my defense, he didn't stay outside as the lookout."

"Even better. You planned to enter alone?"

"Uh, yes?"

Jonah shook his dark head. "No more, Addie. I'm serious. Promise me."

"I was careful."

"Promise me. And clearly you weren't," he added, pointing to his splint.

"One little bullet. You're never going to let me forget that, are you?" She sighed. "I promise. I never meant for that to happen, Jonah." Tears threatened, and she sniffed them back.

"I know. Please don't cry."

She grinned. "Okay."

He shook his head again. "Never going to be easy with you."

"Nope. I know the company that organized the sale. I could give them a call tomorrow, see if there's anything else of interest left."

"That's a good idea. And safe. I like it when you have ideas that don't involve gunshots and arson."

"Me, too."

"If I ask you something, Addie, do you promise to tell me the truth?"

"When have I ever lied to you?"

"Well, not so much lied as maybe didn't tell me everything."

"Oh. That. I promise."

"Did you dream about this before it happened?"

She nodded. "Only once. The night before the estate sale."

"And you didn't tell me."

She shredded her paper towel. "No. I didn't know what it meant yet. And I didn't want to seem like a freak." She dropped her chin, staring at the pile of napkin bits before her.

"Addie." He raised her chin with a finger under it. "I don't understand why you dream, or even what they mean. But I need you to share them with me. Not hold back. Maybe together, we can figure them out."

Her breath came out in a rush. She hadn't even known she'd been holding it. "I don't understand any of it. It would be nice to share them with someone. With you."

"Agreed. Next time, don't hold back." He balled up the foil from his tacos. "Now, why don't we watch a movie?"

"I happen to own everything made by Monty Python," she joked.

"*Holy Grail,* it is."

*****

Several hours later, after watching not only *Holy Grail* but *Life of Brian* as well, Addie glanced at his sleeping face. And marveled at how far they'd come in such a short time. When they first met, her covered in blood in a neighbor's driveway, she'd thought him stoic. Maybe even a little stiff. But then again, he was a detective, and she was covered in a stranger's blood. A dead stranger's blood.

A few months later, here they were on her couch. With his overnight bag tossed in the corner of the living room. Life was good.

Jonah yawned, then sat up straighter. "Sorry."

"You missed the last half of the second movie."

Her phone chirped, indicating a text. She picked it up, opening the message. And laughed. "Grey and Jamie didn't win. But they do look cute." She turned the phone for him to see.

"Who are they supposed to be?"

"Caesar and Brutus."

"Wow, pretty high brow for Halloween."

That made her laugh harder. "He wanted to wear a toga."

"Oh."

She caught him staring at her. "What?"

"I like it when you laugh."

"If life would calm down, I'd laugh more."

"It will. You will." He leaned in and kissed her. A sweet kiss that spoke of the future. "I promise."

"I like the sound of that." She tried to smother a yawn. "That had nothing to do with you."

"I won't take it personally. It's been a long day. I'm going to take a shower." He stood, kissing her head before heading into her bedroom.

"Okay, girls, last potty trip tonight."

They followed her to the kitchen slider. She smiled thinking about Jonah in her shower. How far they'd come. Last night, a whole herd of butterflies had taken up residence in her stomach. Now, she was an old pro. Not nervous at all.

Well, maybe just a little.

She let the girls back in and locked up before heading into her room. Jonah met her on his way from the bathroom. "All yours."

"Thanks. I won't be long." She grabbed her pajamas from a drawer and headed in, closing the door behind her. Excited to sleep next to him again, she rushed through her nightly routine.

She climbed into bed next to him, kissing him before turning out the light. As if she'd done it a million times. Not just one. And lay awake, once again, despite the long day.

"I can hear you thinking over here."

Addie turned her head to see him. "What did you want to be when you were in kindergarten?"

A bark of laughter sounded in the otherwise silent room. "That's what you were thinking?"

"No, I was thinking how I should be tired. But I'm not."

"Because I'm in your bed."

She noted the lack of a question mark at the end of that. "Well, yes." She cleared her throat and resisted the temptation to do something with her hands. "Don't you find this odd?"

"This? You mean lying in bed with you?"

"No, the fact that Aunt Beatrice thinks blue hair is normal. Yes, the fact that you're in my bed."

"Would it be easier if you were in mine?"

She threw up her hands and rolled away from him onto her side. And didn't answer.

"A firefighter."

"What?"

"When I was in kindergarten, I wanted to be a firefighter. I thought they all lived in the station with a Dalmatian. Sliding down the shiny pole clinched it."

"Then your father died."

"Then my father died. And all thoughts of being a firefighter fled."

She rolled onto her other side, facing him. She could just see his face in the dim moonlight filtering through her curtains. "You need a haircut." She reached out and pushed a thick lock of hair out of his eyes.

"Are you offering?"

Her light laugh floated in the air. "Trust me, you don't want that." She sighed. "I miss Gwen."

Her friend and hairdresser, Gwen Tucker, was murdered last month by past associates from New York City. Gwen had worked as an accountant for a mob shell company. She'd moved to Ocean Grove five years ago as part of the Witness Protection Program. They'd found her.

Jonah grasped her hand. "I know you do."

She squeezed his hand, grateful for the support. "I need to find another place to get my hair cut. It's time."

"And you can take me with you."

"I can." Her eyes grew heavy. She inched closer to him, resting her cheek on his chest. "I'm not hurting you, am I?"

He wrapped his arm around her. "I've got you. Go to sleep."

And she did.

Chapter Nine

"Where is Jonah? Don't hurt him. Please. I'll tell you whatever you want to hear."

"Of course, you will, my dear." He clucked his tongue. "Sadly, it's too late for your friend." His gentle tone belied his words.

"No," Addie cried. Fat, hot tears poured down her cheeks. She couldn't have lost him. Not when she just found him. She pulled at the rope binding her wrists, but they held fast. Her eyes darted around the ornate room. There must be something she could use as a weapon.

"Addie! Wake up."

Addie sat straight up in bed, her chest heaving with the effort to breathe. Pale light, suggesting dawn, bathed the room. "Jonah!" She threw her trembling arms around him and hugged him as hard as she could. "You're okay."

A muttered oath from him reminded her of his injured arm. She backed away, releasing him. Her hand flew to her mouth. "I'm so sorry. Did I hurt you?"

He rubbed his left arm. "Only a little." The dimple appeared when he grinned. "A little pain was worth that enthusiasm."

She ducked her head when warmth spread across her cheeks. "I thought you were dead."

Jonah gathered her against his chest. "Another bad dream?" he guessed.

She nodded against him. "The worst yet. He told me you were dead. I couldn't find you anywhere."

Jonah hugged her tighter to him. "I'm fine, Addie. I'm right here with you," he murmured against her hair.

She straightened up, dashing tears from her face. "I got you wet."

"I'll survive. Tell me about the dream."

Gracey stood up from her bed and stretched before walking to the side of the bed. She stretched her neck upwards and whined. Lily followed suit, going to Jonah's side of the bed. He reached down and scratched behind one silky ear. After a few seconds, both dogs headed to the bedroom door.

Addie got out of bed. "Welcome to life with dogs. I'll be right back."

She walked into the kitchen. The chilly floor tiles curled her toes. Fall was here for sure. She let the girls into the yard before grabbing things from the fridge to make them breakfast. Not that she was avoiding Jonah. Or talking about the nightmare. Just being a good hostess.

Yeah, right!

She cracked the eggs into a bowl. With more force than needed. And whipped them. Humming an old tune her Aunt Clementine taught her, she added rye bread to the toaster. Turning back to the stove, she poured the eggs into one pan and placed bacon in another. She stirred the eggs, praying they didn't burn this time.

"Are you avoiding me?"

"Gah!" She dropped the spatula and whirled. "Ten years, Jonah, right off the top."

He tried, without a lot of success, to smother a laugh. "I'm sorry. Did you forget I was here? In your house?"

"No, of course not. I didn't expect you to sneak up on me though."

"Sneak? Don't you think I'm a bit big for sneaking?"

She looked him up and down. He had a point. At over six feet and close to two hundred pounds of solid muscle, he wasn't a ninja. "Good point." She turned back to the stove. "I hope you like scrambled. It's all I know."

"I like anything I don't have to make myself," he assured her before closing the gap between them. Jonah swept her hair off her neck and placed a kiss at the nape. "I will love anything you want to make for me. Although, Grey did warn me about your culinary skills."

The zings travelled down her spine. "Oh, did he? Grey is a compulsive liar. Although, in this case, he's right." She huffed a bit. "In my defense, I can handle eggs and bacon. And pasta. I'm not bad at that either."

"I'm happy to cook for you when I can." He waved his splint. "Only a few more days until I can say goodbye, and good riddance, to this."

She smiled. "And you know what that means."

He wagged his eyebrows. "I hope so."

She nodded. "Yep, your turn to cook."

She shrieked as he wrapped his good arm around her and nuzzled the sensitive spot on her neck. "The bacon is going to burn."

"I'll risk it," he growled into her neck, making her laugh.

A riot of barking sounded at the slider. Both turned to find the girls pressed nose first into the glass, barking at him.

"Grey isn't my only watch dog, as you can see."

She wiggled out of his grasp and went to open the door. The girls ran in, swarming around her legs. She pet them before returning to the stove.

Jonah sat at the table and whistled for them. Two sets of ears swiveled. Gracey and Lily ran to his outstretched hand. "Now girls, we're going to have to come to an understanding about your mom."

She melted, watching the big, tough detective talk to her silly little dogs in a sing-song voice. She stirred the eggs and flipped the bacon, concentrating on the task at hand. Couldn't reward him for his kindness to the girls by serving burnt food.

He waited until they were both seated and digging into breakfast. "Why don't you tell me about the dream that had you crying out in your sleep?"

She sighed and stopped buttering a piece of bread. "It was awful, Jonah. I couldn't find you. And that man, the one who keeps showing up, told me it was too late for you." She took a breath. "I couldn't find you, Jonah."

"I'm right here, Addie, and I'm not going anywhere. Soon, I'll be back to normal. I don't want you to worry about me."

"How can I not? The dream seemed so real. They always do."

"How about this? We promise to take care of each other, not take chances, and be safe."

She let out a shuddery breath. "I can do that."

"Good. Now tell me about this estate sale company."

"The company is called Worthington Estate Sales and Auctions. I didn't know the staff on Saturday, but I've run into that company many times in the past. They have a solid reputation in the business."

"Okay, that's good. Do you have a contact? Someone you could call about the Abernathy estate?"

"Sure. The owner, Claire Worthington, is a doll to deal with. In fact, I was surprised not to find her at the sale."

"We have a place to start. Good."

"'We'. I like the sound of that," she replied with a smile.

He poured juice for them. She smiled at him. For just this moment in time, life seemed normal. She'd take it.

*****

Monday morning dawned bright and nippy. Just the way Addie liked her fall days. She and Jonah whiled Sunday away, reading the paper and arguing about college football on TV. Coming from Georgia, he was, regrettably, a dyed in the wool Bulldogs fan. On the other hand, she bled Carolina Blue. They ate all their meals together, and she fell asleep with his arm draped over her. No nightmares to break the peace. Life felt pretty much perfect. Except, of course, for that pesky, vaguely threatening man. And the disturbing flowers.

She dropped Jonah off at his home before heading to the store early. As much as she loved her customers, she enjoyed the hours before she opened the store. It gave her time to tidy up and catch up on things. She pulled around the back and parked in her usual spot. Glancing in the rear-view mirror, she smiled at the girls. Asleep ten seconds ago, they stood now, whining to get out.

"Okay, okay. Hold on to your fur," she called to them.

Grabbing her purse, she exited and let the girls out. They pranced around, noses lifted to the air. The delicious scents coming from The Daily Grind next door tempted her to do the same. The coffee joint specialized in holiday brews. The scent of pumpkin spice drifted towards her.

Entering through the rear door, Addie stopped to turn off the alarm before letting the dogs off their leashes. Gracey and Lily ran behind the counter. She followed at a slower pace. Something out of the corner of her eye stopped her in her tracks. A large stuffed bear sat outside the front door, propped against it. With leaden steps, she approached the door, staring down at the stuffed animal. She craned her neck to look in either direction on the street. A few early morning exercisers walked by. Otherwise, the street sat empty.

With acid swirling in her gut, Addie unlocked the door and opened it. The bear, more than three feet high of stuffed softness, tumbled backwards and landed on her feet. The large red bow around its neck held a card like the one in her flowers. With her foot, she pushed the bear into the store before relocking the door. She squatted down to read the card. 'I can't bear to be without you,' followed by a heart.

The sudden chill she felt had nothing to do with the calendar. Addie pulled her phone from her back pocket. And hit a preset. After a few rings, Jonah's voice came over.

"Hey. Miss me already?"

"No. I mean yes, but that's not why I'm calling."

He swore under his breath as she told him about her latest gift. "Don't touch anything. I'll be right there."

He'd disconnected before she could protest. Not that she would have. Gifts from her unknown admirer creeped her out. She took a picture of the offending bear and texted it to Grey. Unwilling to let the 'gift' unnerve her further, she pulled it to her office and shut the door on it. She then went behind the corner and gave the girls their breakfast. With their crunching as background music, Addie booted up her laptop. She glanced at her phone. Only a little after eight. She'd wait a little to call Claire at the estate sale company.

Her phone emitted the scary ghost sound announcing a call from Grey. She slid her finger across to answer and hit speaker.

"What the hell, Addie?" resounded in the empty store.

"Right? I used to love bears as a child." She shivered. "Not anymore."

"Understandable. The question is what Detective Hottie is going to do about his competition."

"First, stop calling him that. You might slip up one day in front of him. Second, mystery man is no competition. Jonah is real. And sweet. And funny."

"Ooh, you had sex with him. Finally!"

"No, I didn't - not that it's any of your business."

"Oh. So, this is serious, then."

"Very."

"Should I dust off my tux? I do look smashing in it."

"No and yes."

"Okay. I'm on my way in. And by that, I mean I'm out of bed. Give me an hour." He ended on a yawn.

"Ninety minutes, it is."

"Love you. And don't open the door for any strange men."

"I won't. Love you more." She disconnected before he could say 'to the moon and back.' It was a thing for them.

She sat on her stool and opened her Internet browser. Typing 'Henry Abernathy' in the search engine, Addie wondered if anything about buried treasure would appear. Thousands of hits appeared. She made her way through them, most dealing with the family name and philanthropy. Several pages in, she found a link for the name and 'mystery of the buried treasure'. Intrigued, she clicked the link.

A television show about mysteries had attempted to interview Mr. Abernathy about his belief in a lost buried treasure. The host reported reluctance on the old man's part. And a lot of speculation about the existence of the treasure, rumored to be pirate plunder from a long-ago sunken galleon.

"Wow. Wait until Uncle Grey hears about this."

Lily woofed at the mention of her second favorite person. Addie laughed. "Hold your fur. He'll be here before you know it."

I Need a Hero sounded from her phone. Grey's pick of the month for Jonah's text alert.

"I'm outside."

She jumped off the stool and raced to the door, not bothering to answer. Unlocking it, she opened it wide, delighted to see him.

It's barely been an hour. Don't be that girl.

"Hey," she said, striving for casual.

His dark gaze swept past her, searching the store.

"Come in. I put it in my office." She led the way. The girls, excited for company, raced out from behind the desk, almost tripping Jonah in their fervor.

"Hello, girls. It's only been a little bit." Nevertheless, he leaned down, scratching each behind their ears before following Addie.

She pushed open the door of her office with a foot. And there sat the bear. It didn't look soft and cute. Just unwanted and a bit sinister.

Jonah walked around it before squatting down to read the card still attached to its ribbon. His face hardened. "Really? I've had enough."

He shut the door and pulled out his phone. She stood, chewing on her bottom lip as he placed a call to Dan. The call lasted a minute.

When he ended it, Jonah approached her. He laced his good hand through her curls, anchoring her to him. And branded her with a short, intense kiss that left her boneless.

"I don't like this. Not one bit. You're mine." Goosebumps raised on her arms at the intensity of his words. And the look in his dark eyes.

"And you are mine."

He nodded. "Glad we have that settled. Dan is on his way to collect the evidence. Think I'll hang around here today, if you don't mind."

"Smoking hot tough guy wants to keep me company and safe? What's not to love?"

One corner of his mouth raised. "'Smoking hot', huh?"

"Yes. Just don't let it go to your head."

"Where's your watchdog?"

"On his way. He was my second call."

A genuine smile lit Jonah's face. "Good."

They walked back to the front of the store. "Take a look at what I found." Turning her laptop towards him, Addie pointed to the article she'd been reading.

"Wait until Grey reads this," he muttered. "There'll be no living with him."

She laughed. "Great minds and all that. I thought the same thing." She glanced at the time. "I'm going to call Claire. See if she can help us at all." She searched through her contacts, pressing the one for the estate sale company. It rang several times before the voicemail message started. She waited until the beep to leave a message and her number before ending the call. "Best I can do for now."

"Mind if I borrow your computer? I'd like to do a bit of my own research."

"Of course not. I'm going to do some stocking while we wait for Grey."

Addie buried herself in the task, bringing out new stock. She loved this part of her job. Getting to see new books by favored authors made her day. Way better than paperwork. She forgot all about time until the girls woofed from behind the counter.

"What did I miss?" asked Grey, coming through the front door.

"Nothing much. I left a message for the estate sale company owner. Maybe she can give us more information." She took the coffee he held out to her. "Thank you."

Grey laughed. "No thanks necessary. We all know what you're like before caffeine." He turned to Jonah, handing him a cup. "I guess you're finding out as well. Have no idea how you like yours. I went with black. There's cream and sugar in the bag."

"Thanks. And for the future, I like it any way other than brewed at the station." He wrinkled his nose. "That rot could burn a hole right through your gut."

"Duly noted. And don't think I missed you skipping right over the part where I implied you've been at Addie's before coffee."

"I wouldn't expect any less."

Addie held up a hand. "Boys! Do I have to send you to separate corners?" She covered a laugh by taking a sip of the delicious smelling pumpkin spiced coffee.

"He started it," mumbled Jonah.

"I expect better of you. Don't let him corrupt you."

"Hey! I resemble that remark," quipped Grey.

"Exactly."

"Only one person in this room is allowed to corrupt me."

She grinned at Jonah. "Ah, you say the sweetest things."

"Geez. Here we go again with the mushiness. Get a room."

"Pipe down, Grey."

"Anyone home?" came a male voice as the door swung open.

Jonah turned to greet Dan. "Hey, thanks for coming."

"No problem. Can't have someone stalking our woman."

"My woman," he growled.

"You know what I mean. Where's the bear in question?"

"In my office. Follow me." Opening the door, she pointed at the stuffed animal.

The detective let out a low whistle. "Wow. Someone really has the hots for you."

"Do you mind?" asked Jonah with more than a hint of steel to his voice.

Dan laughed. "Overprotective much?" He pulled a pair of gloves from his pocket. Unknotting the ribbon tied around the bear's neck, he slid it and the card into a plastic evidence bag. "I'll take this back with me to check for prints."

"Aren't you going to take that?"

He glanced at the bear. "Miss Foster, there's not a lot to be gained from that. I can take note of the manufacturer, call around to see who might have bought one. It's a long shot, to be frank." He grimaced. "You don't want to hear this, but there hasn't been a crime committed."

"Yet," added Grey.

"Someone has to hurt me first?"

"That's great," grunted Grey, taking a step closer to this BFF. "They'll have to get through me first."

Jonah sighed. "Hold up, everyone. Dan is right. There hasn't been a crime."

"Not you, too," grumbled Grey.

"By the letter of the law, leaving an oversized bear at the front door isn't a crime."

"Maybe not, but it is creepy." Addie shuddered at the thought of someone skulking in the middle of the night outside her shop.

"May not be illegal, but that doesn't make it right."

"I agree, Grey. Even though a crime hasn't been committed, I'm not letting this go." Jonah inched closer to Addie.

She turned to him, wearing a frown. "Because you don't think this is going to stop."

"No." He reached for her hand. "I don't."

The solid feel of his hand gave her strength. She wasn't alone in this. He took this seriously. "Okay, then. What do we do?"

Chapter Ten

"That's my cue. I'll take this back to the station. Do what you want with that," Dan gestured to the bear, slumped over on the floor at his feet. "I'll call you, Jonah, when I have anything."

"Thank you, Detective. Let me walk you out." Addie led him to the door, locking it again after he left. She turned to see the two men in her life with their heads together. While their getting along better pleased her, the sight did nothing to comfort her.

"Okay, you two, out with it." They sprang apart at her words.

"I have no idea what you're talking about, Addie," protested Grey. "Luckily for you, I have a thick skin. And a burning need to tidy up before opening." He grabbed his coffee before wandering around the store.

"That leaves you, Mister."

Jonah's wide-eyed expression left her laughing but not convinced of his innocence.

"Spill."

"Fine. If you must know, we discussed what to do with that." He nudged the bear with his foot. "I informed Grey that burning it in the town square wasn't an option."

"Darn."

"You, too?"

"Well, it would send a message."

"And get you arrested."

"Would that involve handcuffs?"

*****

At lunch, Addie watched Jonah over her cheeseburger. The movement of his jaws as he chewed and swallowed fascinated her. Then shook her head.

There's something very wrong with her.

"Still thinking about my handcuffs?" he asked before wiping his mouth.

"Maybe," she stammered. Better for him to think that than the fact that her obsession with him grew daily. She put down the rest of her burger. "Grey, are you okay with holding down the fort for a bit?"

"As long as you're not expecting a wave of ankle biters."

"Not until tomorrow. I'll be back by then."

"In that case, I'm good. What's up?"

"Claire returned my call while you were out picking up lunch. She's able to meet us at the estate this afternoon."

"I wanna go."

"If you're about to stomp your foot, don't. Someone has to stay here."

"Jonah can stay. Even with one arm, he can watch the store."

Jonah waved his good hand. "I'm right here."

Grey grinned. "See? He can do it."

"Jonah doesn't work here."

"Then deputize him or something."

Addie sighed. "You're watching too many old Westerns again. Besides, I'd like Jonah to come with me. Then I can be alone with him in the car. But you can keep the girls if you want."

"Fine. But I used to be your first choice."

Addie walked over to him, throwing her arms around his waist. "You're still my favorite BFF."

"I'm the only one you have."

Jonah glanced up from his seat. "Did you guys want a moment alone?"

Addie's laugh trickled through the room. "Nope. We're fine. Aren't we, Grey?"

"I suppose. But one night soon, it's you and me and way too many margaritas." He glared at Jonah. "Like in the good old days."

"You're on." She kissed his cheek and grabbed her coat. "Let's go. Remember, Grey, be nice to the customers."

"If I have to."

She had nothing to worry about. Grey could charm the birds from the trees. Sell ice to Eskimos. People loved him and his outrageous sense of humor.

"Thank you. We shouldn't be too long."

She walked behind the counter. "Okay, girls, you'll be staying with Uncle Grey for a bit. Be on your best behavior." She kissed both girls on their silky heads before tossing them each a treat.

"Let's go."

They walked through the back entrance to the alley behind the store. Once they both buckled their seat belts, she backed out of her space. Jonah grabbed for the handle as she took the corner a bit quickly. She glanced at his face and tried not to laugh.

"Have a problem with my driving?"

"No, of course not. Well, except the part where I think we're going to die. That, I could do without."

"I'll have you know, I have a clean record."

"I know."

She glanced at him as she stopped at a red light. "You do?"

"Of course."

"Oh, right. When you suspected me of murder."

"Yep."

She punched his thigh, then pulled into the intersection.

"What was that for?"

"You didn't have to agree with me. But I knew it! I knew you suspected me in the beginning."

"Not really. More of a formality. What with you being the first on the scene and all."

"Hey! I could totally have been the murderer."

He held up his good hand to ward her off. "Don't punch me again."

"I wasn't going to. At least tell me why not."

He shook his head. "First you're mad because I called you a suspect. Then you're mad because I didn't think of you as one. Which is it?"

"Sure, bring logic into it. Tell me why you don't think I could have done it."

"Addie, you fainted at the sight of blood on you."

"In my defense, there was a lot of it." She shuddered at the memory of that morning last summer. She'd rushed into the darkened garage, thinking she could help the person lying there. But he was dead. Very dead. She'd slid in his spilled blood, landing in it.

"Yes, I knew pretty much right then and there, despite your being covered in blood."

"What did you think of me?"

His head snapped in her direction. "That first moment?"

"Yes. I'm intrigued."

He laughed a bit, like maybe he didn't like being put on the spot.

She felt the tiniest bit sorry. "Forget it."

"I thought you were very brave. And gorgeous. Despite being covered in blood."

She loosened her grip on the wheel. "Oh. Really?"

"You made me laugh. That attitude in your voice when I called you 'ma'am'."

"I am coming up on a big birthday."

"Age is a number, Addie. You're only as old as you feel."

"I felt about ninety that day."

"Hmmm. Go ahead, I can take it."

"Take what?"

"Tell me what you thought of me. That first day we met."

"I felt safe."

He made a face, telling her what he thought of that.

"After finding a dead body and being covered in his blood, safe was a great thing. You made me feel safe, Jonah. As if I didn't have to worry anymore."

His face softened. "I can live with that."

"Grey found you handsome."

"Lovely."

"Not in a hitting on you way, silly goose. He commented on you and I and what, uh, never mind." She focused on the road, willing Jonah to ignore what she almost said.

"You and I what?"

She took a deep breath, letting it out slowly. "He, uh, mentioned what pretty babies we'd make." She risked a glance. And saw his jaw hit the floor of the car. She rushed on. "Consider the source though. Grey is desperate for me to have a baby. Really doesn't matter who the father is."

"He's not wrong."

And then *her* jaw dropped. "That is not what I expected to hear."

A chuckle escaped him. "Clearly. I'm not suggesting a pack of them right now. Just, you know, something to consider. For down the road."

How she kept the car on the road was anyone's guess. "Good to know." The GPS on her phone announced the turnoff. She slowed and made the turn, then headed down the long, treelined lane.

"Did I freak you out? That wasn't my intention."

Her heart sank at his formal tone. This was how he spoke to her in the beginning, all stiff. "I'm not freaked out. Maybe surprised a little." She glanced at him. "I guess I'm not used to this."

"To what?"

"You're very direct."

"Life is short. Without guarantees. When you care about someone, you should tell them." He turned to face her. "I care for you, Addie, about you. A lot."

She waited to respond until she pulled in next to the house and shut off the engine. She turned to him. "I care about you, too, Jonah. More than you know." Her pulse throbbed in her throat.

"I 'll keep you safe, Addie. No one's going to hurt you."

"I believe you."

"Good. Now, let's go figure out this mess."

"Sounds like a plan."

A red pickup truck, bearing the name Worthington Estate Sales, pulled in next to them. Addie waved to the older woman at the wheel before getting out of her car and walking towards Claire.

"Addie!"

Older than her by a good fifteen years, Claire Worthington looked a decade younger. Tall and trim, she had an athletic grace from years of riding. She ran the Southern division of the family business.

"HI, Claire. Come meet Jonah Wolfe. Jonah, this is Claire Worthington, the owner of Worthington Estate sales."

The two exchanged greetings. Claire then turned her inquisitive gaze back to Addie. "You certainly caught my attention on the phone. Tell me more about what's going on."

Addie caught her up on what had happened. Tension radiating from Jonah at her side, but he remained quiet. When she finished, Claire frowned. "I cannot release the name of any of my customers. My business depends upon discretion. And professionalism."

"I can produce a warrant," replied Jonah.

Claire smiled at him. "Then by all means, please do." She turned to Addie. "You didn't tell me your friend was a police officer."

"That's 'Detective', Ms. Worthington."

"It wouldn't matter if you were the chief, Detective Wolfe. I will not release any of my client's information without a warrant." She smiled at Addie. "But I am more than happy to allow you into the library today to have another look."

"And we appreciate that."

She dug into her oversized handbag. "Ah, here they are." She held up a set of keys. "Shall we?"

They followed her to the main entrance. Once inside, Addie soaked in the beauty of the two-story foyer. "This view never gets old," she murmured, almost reverently.

'One perk to this job is getting to see old beautiful houses such as this. Mind you, very few of our properties match the

Abernathy estate." She grinned at Addie. "I wouldn't mind calling this place home myself."

"Right?" She glanced around her as they proceeded down the hall to the library. And sighed. "Mind you, if I lived here, I'd never want to leave."

Jonah scoffed. "Never go to the beach again? Or go shopping with Grey?"

"I guess. But still, imagine owning such a beautiful old house."

"Well, if you have several million lying around, the estate goes on the market soon." She opened the door into the library.

Addie entered, as thrilled with the room as she had been the first time. "This room alone would be worth the price of admission. Sadly, I'm several million short." She grinned at Jonah. "But Grey isn't. Maybe I can talk him into buying it for me. My birthday is right around the corner." She turned to Jonah, expecting him to laugh at her outrageous comment. But his mouth flattened into a hard line.

"Uh, anyway, do you know if there were any additional boxes found in the cellar, Claire?"

"I don't believe so. Just the ones you saw that morning. What is it exactly you're looking for?"

"Anything worth coming after Addie for," commented Jonah. He glanced around the room. "May as well be a needle in a haystack."

Addie followed his gaze. "You have no idea. There were hundreds more books here on Saturday morning." She gnawed on her bottom lip. "Where would we even start?"

"Why don't you start here, Addie? I'll take a walk through, make sure nothing's been left behind."

"Sounds like a plan, Claire. Thank you."

She watched the other woman walk out of the room then turned to Jonah. "Are you okay?" She reached out a hand to soothe the tautness of his jaw. Her heart squeezed when he leaned his jaw into her hand.

After a moment, he straightened. "When Grey buys this place for you, can I visit?"

And her heart squeezed tighter. "Oh, Jonah, surely you know I'm joking."

He stared at her for so long, she grew afraid of what he might be thinking. "I'm a detective, Addie; not a trust fund baby. I do alright, but I could never buy this for you."

"And I would never want you to. Have you met me? I wear flip flops, not Jimmy Choos. My idea of haute cuisine is Chef Henri's special macaroni au fromage. And besides, who'd want to clean a house this big? I can barely manage my place."

"If you can afford to live here, you can afford a cleaning crew. Not to mention a chauffeur and personal chef."

"I love my little house. And my flip flops. And my life." *And you,* she didn't quite add. Too soon for that. But the vulnerable side of him melted her heart. She looked him in the eye, making sure he heard her. "I love my life. I have everything I could ever want."

One corner of his mouth lifted. "Me, too."

It was the perfect moment. Until a blood curdling scream ripped the air.

Chapter Eleven

"Claire?" Addie yelled as she ran to the library doors. The shrieking echoed through the old home. It could be coming from anywhere.

Jonah dashed in front of her. "Stay here."

"What? You aren't even armed."

Before they could argue about it, Claire ran into the library, eyes bulging. "B-B-Betty needs h-h-help." She raised a shaking hand to point back the way she'd come.

Addie pulled her phone from her pocket, ready to call for help. But she didn't know what kind of help they needed.

Jonah placed a hand on Claire's shoulder. "Take a deep breath and tell me what happened."

Tears rolled down her face as she spoke. "I found Betty Nelson, one of my employees. I think she's dead." She closed her eyes and shook her head. "Her head is at a terrible angle. And her eyes." She sobbed harder. "She stared right through me." She stopped talking, burying her head in Jonah's chest.

He looked at Addie over the older woman's head. "Call 9-1-1. Tell them there's a dead body, most likely foul play. Give them my name."

She nodded and did as he asked. The dispatcher asked her many questions. She answered as best she could. Then she disconnected. "They're sending help."

"Good." He pat Claire on the shoulder. "Miss Worthington, I need to ask you some questions. Can you help me out?"

She raised her red-rimmed eyes. "What? Oh yes, you're a detective. I forgot." She straightened up even as a shudder ran through her body. "Yes, of course. I've never seen a dead body before."

"You can start by telling me what happened," Jonah stated in that gentle voice he'd used with her before.

"I, uh, walked through the house, room by room, to make sure there weren't any other boxes of books. After I left the two of you, I decided the best way to proceed would be to start at the top and make my way down. I didn't find anything. I even looked in the basement, as that's where the boxes had been discovered." She took a breath, letting it out slowly. "I came back up from the cellar. That's when I remembered the office, so to speak."

"What do you mean?"

"There's a small room, not an office, really, more of a pantry. Adjacent to the kitchen. We, my staff and I, used it as an office when we set up the estate sale. We used a couple of folding tables and chairs. I sat in there, cataloguing furniture and the like for days prior to the sale." Fresh tears coursed down her face. "That's where I found her, Betty, lying on the floor. Staring."

"That can't have been easy for you. Can you tell me where this room is?"

"Go right out the door to the end of the hall. It's the door before you head into the kitchen. It's the only one open."

"Addie, take Claire outside to wait for the police, please. I'm going to have a look."

She nodded. "Claire, come along with me. Some fresh air will do you good." The other woman nodded and allowed herself to be led like a small child.

The three of them left the library. Addie stopped to watch Jonah head away from them down the hall. She wanted to go with him, but Claire's ice-cold hand clutched her wrist.

"Let's go outside."

She led her outside, wondering what Jonah would find. Addie shivered against the light autumn breeze, wishing for the flannel jacket in her car. She made small talk with Claire, anything to keep the other woman's mind occupied.

Jonah joined them in the circular drive as a Brunswick County Sheriff's car pulled up. He walked past the two women to greet the officer. Addie watched him shake hands and point towards Claire. They approached.

"Ms. Worthington, this is Deputy Jeffries from the sheriff's department. He has some questions for you."

She stepped forward. "Of course. Thank you, Deputy, for respondingso quickly."

An ambulance and black van joined the other cars in the driveway. Then more came. Before she could blink, scores of people milled about, taking photographs and talking in hushed tones. Addie walked back inside and sat on the bottom step of the grand stairway. For once, she didn't exist at the center of the controversy. She hadn't even found the body. And was thankful. Then winced. Betty had been nice to her on Saturday morning. She didn't deserve this cruel end. She settled in to wait.

Over an hour later, Jonah crossed the foyer towards her. "There you are." He leaned in for a quick kiss. "Sorry, I lost track of time."

"No worries." Her mouth turned down. "She's really dead, huh?"

He nodded. "Did you know her well?"

"No. I met her Saturday. But she was kind to me, offering me the boxes of books." She sat up straighter. "This must all be connected. Right? That man who approached me and then in the shop. And Betty's death. It's the only way it makes sense. And for what? A stupid treasure that most likely doesn't exist." She stood and paced, her boot heels clicking along the hardwood floor.

"I see what you're doing, Addie Foster. What you're thinking. Stop. This is not your case. It's not even mine."

And she did stop. Right in front of him. And poked him in the chest. "Don't you see? That man, whoever he is, isn't going to stop. Not when he believes there's buried treasure and somehow the books hold the key to it."

"You may be right. But you're a bookstore owner, not a detective. And I am a detective but on leave. And this is way outside of my jurisdiction." He held up a hand when she would have said something. "I've given them Dan's information. And yours and mine. It's the best I can do. Now, let's go."

She would have argued, but he was right. Darn him.

She placed her hand in his and tugged. "You're right. Let's go."

Jonah rolled his eyes. "Do I look stupid to you?"

"What? No, of course not. Why?"

"Nice try. I can hear the wheels spinning in your head. You're planning something. God knows what. You may as well tell me now."

She looked around the foyer. Police and various techs still mingled. "You're right. Why don't we head home?"

His eyes lit up. "Good idea. I'll say goodbye." He walked off, speaking to a few of the people.

Addie headed outside. Dark, ominous clouds gathered in the sky. The wind had picked up, sending leaves swirling around her ankles.

Very Halloween, but also creepy. She rubbed her arms.

She didn't see Claire anywhere. Her company truck sat empty. Maybe they'd taken her somewhere. Or maybe she remained inside.

She turned at the sound of the front door opening. Jonah's boots crunched across the gravel drive. He smiled at her, that dimple flashing, and it felt as though the sun had peeked out from behind the gathering clouds.

She rushed to greet him. "Hey," she cried before tucking her arm around his waist.

"I was only gone a moment." But his handsome face lit. "I missed you, too." He glanced at the sky. "Let's head out before that opens up on us."

"You read my mind."

She grabbed his hand and headed for her SUV. Addie pulled around the various official vehicles and headed up the long, tree-lined drive to the main road. Only then did she ask her questions.

"Was Betty strangled? That's what it sounded like from Claire's description. When do you think that poor woman died? She was sweet to me on Saturday. I hate to think of her like that. But the sale ran all weekend, so she had to be alive on Sunday. Otherwise, people would have noticed. Did Claire give up the name of the English man yet? She's going to have to now, I imagine." She stopped and took a huge breath.

"Do you have more questions, or should I start answering?" he asked, with a hint of humor in his voice.

She turned onto the main road, waving a hand at him. "You may begin. I'll have more later."

"Of course, you will. You know I shouldn't be telling you any of this."

"But you will, because you care about me."

"Because you'll bug me otherwise."

She grinned. "That, too."

"You're right about the time of death. The coroner placed it at some time last evening."

"The sale would have ended. I wonder if he waited around all day or came back afterwards." She tapped her fingers on the wheel. "Do you think he acted alone?"

"I don't know for sure if it's *him*. Remember?"

"Well, English guy sure wanted that box of books I bought."

"Which doesn't make him a killer."

She waved a hand in his direction. "Details."

His laughter filled the space. "Probably a good thing you own a bookstore."

"Agreed. And yet he *could* be the killer."

"Yes."

"A ha," she crowed.

"Along with any of thousands of other people. Who else knows about the supposed buried treasure? Mr. Abernathy lived into his eighties and had spent a lifetime talking about it, obsessing about it. Plus, that show you found. The one that tried to interview him for it. And finally, it may not be connected to that at all. Maybe Betty had an enemy."

"Ugh," she cried. "This detective thing is harder than it looks."

"Gee, thanks."

She turned her head for a second and smiled at him. "You know what I mean."

"I do. I also like to give you crap now and again. What do you know about Claire Worthington? Beyond just knowing her from estate sales."

"I've known her for years. She's wonderful." She narrowed her eyes. "Is this because she wouldn't give up her client list? She had a point. She has a reputation to protect."

"She's hiding something."

"It must be difficult. Being a detective and always having to suspect people. I'd hate that."

"Not everyone is good, Addie. They don't all have your heart. Some people, a lot, have bad intentions. That's why I have a job."

"Don't you get tired of that? Thinking everyone is guilty or bad until proven otherwise? It makes me sad. And before you say it, I'm not some Pollyanna who believes the world is a safe place filled with unicorns and rainbows. I know, more than most, how scary the world can be."

"And yet, you haven't let what happened to you color your view of the world. Or of people. It's one of the things I love about you."

Her hands trembled on the wheel. A quick glance told her they were alone on the road.

Good thing…

"One of them? As in, there are more?" she couldn't resist asking. She kept her voice light.

"Do you doubt how I feel about you?"

"No, of course not," she replied without any hesitation. He hadn't said the L-word yet. But then, neither had she. And it had only been a few weeks. And they hadn't even had a real date.

"I love you, Addie Foster."

Chapter Twelve

She pulled off the road and placed the car in park. And remembered to breathe. Then turned to face him. "Me, too." A high-pitched laugh escaped her. "You know what I mean."

He took her hand in his, turning it over and tracing a pattern on the sensitive skin of her palm. "I'm sorry."

"You are?"

"No, I'm not sorry I love you. Or that I told you. I'm sorry I did it while you were driving." He blew out a breath. "I know it hasn't been long. And maybe not the most traditional start to a relationship."

"And we haven't even had a real date yet."

"How did you know I was thinking that?"

"I had the very same thoughts." She leaned in and kissed him. "But those things don't matter, Jonah. At least not to me."

"Nor me. You make me happy. With your little dogs, crazy BFF, penchant for trouble, there's never a dull moment."

"Let's not forget the Aunties."

"How could I forget them?"

"Now that we're dating and you don't think I killed someone, they're going to be all over you. Literally."

He grinned. "Are you trying to scare me off? Not going to happen. I happen to find them interesting."

"That's because they haven't pinched your cheeks yet. And I can't guarantee which set they'll go for."

"Two generations of Foster women after me. Cool."

"We'll see. We could have dinner with them tonight, if you feel like wading right in."

"Sounds good."

She looked at him for a long moment before pulling back on the road. After a mile, she hit the preset for her aunts. Clementine answered on the second ring.

"Is that Adelaide Foster, my long-lost niece?"

Addie rolled her eyes. "I saw you Friday, Aunt Clementine."

"Don't you roll your eyes at us, young lady," chimed in Aunt Beatrice.

Jonah covered his mouth with his good hand, stifling a laugh.

She hit mute. "Did I mention they're psychic?" She took the phone off mute. "Guess who wants to come to dinner tonight? Jonah!"

"You mean that yummy detective who thought you killed that man in the garage?"

"Now, Clementine, he only thought that because she was covered in the man's blood. Give him a break." Beatrice squealed over the line, a loud, high-pitched noise generally reserved for teenaged girls. "Does this mean you're sweet on him, dear?"

"More importantly, does it mean you'll be bringing us a pie?"

"Yes, and yes."

"Well, it's about time. This one is a keeper. See you at six, dear." The line went dead.

"Does that mean what I hope it does? Any Way You Slice It? They have the best pies."

"Of course, they do. I wouldn't go anywhere else. Besides, Gertie and I are great friends."

"Can we get Chocolate Chiffon? Or maybe Key Lime? But then the Lemon Meringue melts in your mouth."

"Did you want to be alone with the pie? And I never choose. Gertie chooses for me."

"Really? Does she do that for everyone?"

She shook her head. "Only the special customers."

"Does that make me a special customer, too? By extension?"

"Not sure. Gertie liked Noah a lot."

Jonah held his hand over his heart. "Wow. That stung." Then he smirked. "I'll have to tell her you and I have zing. And you and Noah didn't."

She gasped, holding in a laugh. "Grey had no right telling you that."

"Well, that is why you ended things with him."

"He didn't like dogs."

"That your final answer?" he joked.

"It's what I told him. He didn't stick around long enough to hear the whole story." She shook her head. "It's probably better that way."

"No man wants to be told there isn't any zing."

"Lucky for you, I won't have to."

"I can't wait to get my arm back."

"Amen." She smacked a palm against her forehead. "I forgot to tell Grey."

"We may as call him now. Let him know."

She nodded and hit the preset for him. The phone rang a few times before his smooth baritone sounded.

"Hey kids, enjoy your field trip?"

"Not exactly." She related the events, stopping for his 'Oh my' every few sentences.

"What a mess. Do you think English guy got his hands on the books we need?"

"Grey! A woman is dead!"

"True, and I'm sorry for that. But this makes figuring out who he is that much more important. If he's willing to kill for them, we need to know who he is. And where he is."

"You cannot assume this man murdered her, as I've already explained to Addie."

"He did."

"And you listened to him?"

"Yes, Gray, I did. We don't have proof that he killed that poor woman."

"But you believe he did."

"Yes."

That earned her a scowl from Jonah.

"Where are you now?"

"On our way back. We're having dinner with The Aunties. Do you want to come?"

"Are you stopping at Any Way You Slice It first?"

"Was there any doubt?"

"Okay, then. What time?"

"Six."

"Perfect. I'll bring the girls."

"See you then."

She glanced at Jonah, who stared straight ahead. "You don't mind, do you?"

"What? Oh, you mean bringing Grey? No. He's growing on me. But he better not hog the pie. "

She laughed. "There'll be enough for everyone."

The miles flew by as they chatted about everything and nothing, getting to know each other better. Before she realized it, they entered Ocean Grove. After another five minutes, they parked in front of the bakery. Jonah reached for her hand when she rounded the truck.

A bell rang over the door, announcing their entrance. Gertie Sanders, third generation baker and current owner, grinned as she came through the swinging doors from the kitchen. "Hey, Addie. Let me guess. Dinner with The Aunties?" She wiped her hands on her apron and extended one towards Jonah. "And you must be Addie's new beau, Detective Wolfe. Nice to meet you."

Jonah shook her hand. "You as well. I've heard a lot about you."

"Hurt her, and they'll never find your body."

Jonah's eyes widened. Addie held her breath. She loved her friends. But they were difficult to predict. Then he threw back his head and laughed.

He nodded to Addie. "I like her."

"He knows I'm not kidding, right?"

"I appreciate your loyalty. I also appreciate a good pie."

"Then for you, I have a new recipe I've been fooling around with. Pumpkin Turtle Pie."

Addie couldn't help laughing. "You have a bit of drool there."

"I get that a lot. Shame it's always for my baked goods. Give me a sec." Gertie disappeared through the swinging door to the back.

"I wish I knew someone to fix her up with."

Jonah raised one brow. "You never struck me as the match-making type."

She wrinkled her nose. "That's because I'm not. Too much can go wrong." She sighed. "But Gertie is such a sweetie, and ridiculously beautiful. I can't figure it out."

He glanced down at her. A smile on his face. "The men in this town must be blind or stupid. Maybe both. I know another woman who fits the description who's just newly off the market."

A fluttering swelled up through her chest. "Ah, Detective, you say the nicest things."

"Cut it out. Us single folk can't take the cuteness," grumbled Gertie. She held the pie box over her head. "Keep it up, and this pie finds another home." Her tinkling laugh belied her words.

Jonah gasped. "You wouldn't."

Gertie glanced between the two before handing him the box. "No, I wouldn't, but only because I love Addie." She wagged a finger at him. "Jury's still out on you."

"Duly noted," he replied. He reached for his wallet, pulling a twenty out of it.

"You may want to keep this one," Gertie advised, handing his change back.

"I just might."

"Might, huh?"

"Good for you, Addie. Keep him on his toes."

"Don't worry. She's made it into an Olympic sport."

"Something tells me you can handle it. Say hello to my favorite octogenarians."

"I will. And thanks for trusting us with your new recipe. It sounds amazing."

"Oh, it will be."

They left the store debating if they'd be able to wait to taste the concoction. Addie waited until they were on the road to answer.

"Only if you value your life," she warned. "The Aunties take their pie very seriously. And you didn't exactly make a good first impression."

"Am I ever going to live that down?"

"Accusing me of murder? Unlikely." She smothered a giggle at his dark expression.

"I never accused you of murder. Per se. You were a person of interest."

"Same thing in their eyes. I wouldn't bring it up."

"Wasn't planning on it." He twisted in his seat to face her. "Are they going to like me? It's important they do."

She would have laughed but for the earnest expression on his face. She placed her hand on his knee. "I love you, Jonah. So, they will, too. Besides, you're a single guy. I'd be worried about Aunt Beatrice hitting on you and the inevitable talk of babies."

"I can handle two old ladies."

She snorted as she pulled into their driveway. "Sure, you can."

An audible gulp formed his only reply.

Chapter Thirteen

"Why are you sitting in the car? Is he afraid to come in? We've forgiven him for accusing you of murder, dear," bellowed Aunt Beatrice from the front door. She patted her blue hair helmet.

"Speak for yourself. I'm not so sure," replied Aunt Clementine.

"I did warn you," added Addie, with a note of glee in her voice.

"I've got this." Jonah exited the car, holding the distinctive purple bakery box in his good hand. Apparently, he wasn't above bribery. "What if I told you Gertie Sanders trusted me with her brand-new Pumpkin Turtle Pie?"

"Well, what are you waiting for? Come on in."

Jonah turned his head, grinning at Addie. "See? Nothing to it."

"You'd like to think."

Grey pulled his jeep in behind Addie's SUV. "The party can start now, I'm here." He walked to the back of his vehicle, letting the girls out of the back. They ran in circles through the yard before stopping at her aunts' feet. "What did I miss?" he asked Addie.

"Nothing much. We just got here. Jonah's about to get grilled."

He held the pie box aloft. "I've got this."

Addie shook her head, watching him approach her aunts.

Grey smirked. "Poor guy doesn't have a clue, does he?"

"Nope. I did try to warn him."

Both followed at a distance, watching Jonah greet her aunts. Clementine took the box from his hand, while Beatrice pinched his cheeks.

"Wait until they grab the other set."

"Grey!"

"Right, like they haven't done that to one of your unsuspecting dates," he scoffed.

"True." She quickened her pace. And arrived in time to see her over six-foot boyfriend being smothered by her barely five-foot elderly Aunt Beatrice. He coughed at the cloud of lavender that always surrounded her.

"Okay, that's enough. Let's not rebreak his arm."

"Poor man, taking a bullet for our Adelaide."

"And I'd do it again, Miss Beatrice."

"Oh, he's good," snarked Grey in her ear.

"Yes, he is."

"Barf."

"Be good," she reprimanded him before bending to greet the girls. They yipped their excitement, winding around her legs for attention. "Yes, I know. Mommy left for several hours," she crooned.

Everyone, human and canine, made their way into the house. Addie watched the scene, her heart full. Everyone she cared for most in the world stood in this very room. Grey approached the stove, where a bubbling pot emitted mouthwatering scents.

"Don't even think about it, Mister."

"What?" Grey asked, eyes wide.

"That hasn't worked since you were still in single digits. Wash up like a civilized person first," admonished Clementine.

"Yes, ma'am." He bestowed a smacking kiss on her cheek before heading to the powder room off the kitchen.

"Scoundrel, that one," she muttered without any heat. "You two may use the other washroom."

"That's our cue, Jonah." She led the way upstairs.

"I'm holding my own, don't you think?"

"I wouldn't claim victory just yet."

They washed their hands and headed back downstairs. Grey already sat at the table. The Aunties bustled around. "Don't try to help," she whispered to him. Addie waited while Jonah pulled out her chair.

When they were both seated, he leaned in. "Why shouldn't I help? Surely, they wouldn't mind."

"Did whispering at the supper table become fashionable?"

"No, Aunt Clementine. Jonah wondered if he should be helping y'all." Grey turned his head, smirking at the detective.

"Do I look feeble to you, Detective Wolfe? Maybe I seem old and infirm, incapable of putting up supper."

Jonah shifted in his seat. "Why, no, ma'am, of course not. But I was raised right."

"Well, okay, then." She bustled to the stove.

"Aunt Clementine, is that your famous beef stew I smell? Could I be that lucky?"

"You are right, young lady."

"And don't forget my award-winning yeast rolls," added Aunt Beatrice. "They go well with the stew.

"Jonah, you're in for a real treat. Auntie B's rolls practically melt in your mouth."

Grey placed a napkin on his lap. "I'm more than ready."

Over the next few minutes, the only sounds coming from the kitchen were the scraping of spoons on bowls and panting of happy Shelties. The Aunties were famous for slipping them treats during dinner.

"Detective Wolfe, what are you doing to keep our great-niece safe?"

Chapter Fourteen

Jonah looked up from his bowl. He wiped his mouth on a linen napkin. "Well, ma'am, I'm currently not on active duty, but the Ocean Grove Police Department is taking this whole situation very seriously. Another detective is searching for the gentleman Addie had the run-in with."

"That's all very good, but I'm referring to her stalker. Have you any leads? Any perps?"

Addie bit back a sigh. Everyone in her family watched too much TV. Jonah, bless him, kept a straight face.

"Now, you know I'm not allowed to discuss an ongoing investigation. But know that we're taking that situation very seriously as well. I'm not about to let anything happen to Addie." He raised her hand to his mouth, kissing her knuckles.

A collective sigh came from her aunts.

And a grunt from Grey.

The rest of the meal passed with conversation centered on Halloween and Thanksgiving. Which led to the inevitable debate over stuffing. The Aunties each made their version every holiday. One had to sample both to stay in their good graces. She sent thanks into the universe for such mundane conversation after the day they'd had.

Everyone oohed and aahed over the pie. Grey and Jonah battled over the last piece for seconds. All was right with her world, at least for this moment.

"Detective Wolfe, why aren't you married at your advanced age?"

She spoke too soon. "Aunt Beatrice, that's not a polite question."

The man in question, who'd been drinking water at the time of the question, coughed and choked for a moment. "Ma'am, please call me Jonah. Hearing 'Detective Wolfe' makes me look for my chief. And the question is perfectly reasonable. I guess I hadn't met the right woman." He smiled at Addie. "Until now."

Aunt Beatrice beamed.

"Do you like children? Sister and I aren't getting any younger. Neither is Addie."

She felt her cheeks burn. *You'd think she'd be used to this by now.* "You really don't have to answer that one."

"Why?" demanded Aunt Clementine. "Don't his parts work?"

Grey covered a laugh with his napkin.

Jonah stared at a spot on the wall. "I assure you my parts are all in working order."

"How do you know?" asked Beatrice. "Do you wear boxers or briefs? I read an article about briefs lowering a man's fertility. Something about his swimmers getting too warm. You don't go in hot tubs, do you?"

Addie stood. "Why don't I get started on the dishes. Jonah, could you help me?" She picked up several dessert plates and marched to the sink.

"Why don't I take the girls outside for a romp?" offered a not helpful Grey. He left with the dogs but not before snickering at Jonah.

"I'm so sorry," Addie hissed to him at the sink. She glanced at him, noting the reddened tips of his ears.

"Somehow, I never saw that coming."

"I did warn you."

"True. But my sperm count?"

She turned her head to hide a laugh that wouldn't be denied. "Funny, they never asked about Noah's underwear preferences."

"I'll take that as a good thing. Maybe they knew you didn't have any zing with him."

"I really need to murder Grey."

Her cell rang as Addie placed a plate in the dishwasher. She dried her hands and pulled it from her back pocket.

"Hello?" She listened before saying, "Yes, of course, I'll be right there." She disconnected and slid her phone back in her pocket before turning to Jonah. "That was my security company. My house alarm is going off. The police have been notified. I have to go."

Jonah caught her arm. "*We* have to go." He pulled out his phone and made a call.

She caught the words, 'Do you believe me now?' before turning away. "I'm sorry to leave in such a rush. We have to go."

Her aunts rose from the table as one. "Of course, dear. Please let us know what happened."

"Do you mind if I leave the girls here?"

"Go," advised Aunt Beatrice. "We'll look after the dears."

Addie rushed out to the back yard, filling Grey in on the details. Jonah followed her. After promising to update him, she headed for her car. After buckling up, she drove the few miles to her home. Turning onto her block, Addie gasped at the sea of emergency lights. Several police vehicles sat parked in front of her home.

She turned to Jonah, gnawing on her lower lip. "When will this ever end?"

"You're not alone, Addie. I'm right here with you. We'll get to the bottom of this."

She brushed at the lone tear trickling down her cheek. "When?" she whispered before exiting the car.

Jonah rushed from his side of the vehicle. He slipped his good hand in hers. "Ready?"

"What choice do I have?"

*****

Several hours later, exhaustion pulled at every fiber of her being as Addie pulled into Jonah's driveway. He'd called in a favor, and a young officer was staying at her place until the locksmith could make it in the morning.

She turned off her car, took a deep breath, and turned to Jonah. "What else can happen?"

"I've learned not to ask." He brushed a lock of hair off her face. "I know it doesn't feel so, but you were lucky. Whoever broke in didn't expect an alarm. It wasn't a professional."

"Small mercies." She willed away the threatening tears. "I'm tired."

"I know you are. Let's get some sleep."

The thought of falling into bed with this wonderful man lifted the gloom a bit. "Let's."

She followed Jonah into his townhouse, still surprised at it despite being a regular visitor. She glanced around the living room, a smile on her face as she took in the comfortable furniture grouping and family pictures on the mantel.

"I always expect a man cave when I walk in."

He raised the brow bisected by a scar. "Man cave? Addie, you've been here more than a few times. Not a single neon bar sign in sight. I'm not twenty-two anymore."

"How are you still single? Aunt Beatrice has a point."

"My parents loved each other until the day my dad died. Laughter and chatter reigned at the table. I remember them dancing in the living room in their bare feet. Of course, I thought they were goofy at the time. Always holding hands, little touches." He reached for her hand. "Now I understand. That's what I want. I'm not interested in settling."

"I get that." Her heart thudded in her chest. "How did I ever find you formal, cold even?"

"You did? Should I be hurt?" The twinkle in his eyes belied his words.

"In the very beginning, when you were calling me 'ma'am.'"

Jonah groaned. "How long am I going to pay for that?"

"We'll see."

He held her gaze and walked toward her until mere inches separated them. "From the first moment I set eyes on you, I felt something. And it wasn't cold."

*****

She couldn't find Jonah. Addie twisted her neck to look around the room. The library at the Abernathy estate no longer held any charm or appeal. The dark, empty fireplace became an angry beast. She couldn't see the whole room from her position. Why couldn't she find him?

"You're too late, my dear, if it's your beau you're searching for." A dry laugh followed those words of doom. The older man's English accent lacked charm. His tone held nothing but derision. "All you had

to do was sell me the box that morning. You could have avoided all this." He shrugged his thin shoulders. *"Neither here nor there now."*

She struggled against the ropes binding her wrists. "Please don't hurt him. I'll give you whatever you want."

"I know you will. But it's too late for you and your friend, I fear." He pulled a dark, menacing gun from the inside pocket of his sports coat.

Tears coursed down her face, dripping onto the expensive rug beneath her. He would shoot her, and Jonah might already be dead. All for a silly pirate treasure that probably was just the stuff of legends.

"Wake up."

The hand on her shoulder dragged her from the depths of her nightmare. She flung herself into Jonah's embrace. "You're alive," she sobbed, sagging against his warm chest.

He gathered her against him, holding her with his good arm, all the while whispering into her hair. "I'm right here, Addie. Don't cry. We're both fine."

Her breathing slowed from its ragged pace. She sighed, settling into him further. "I thought he'd killed you. He scared me, waving the gun, telling me it was too late for you."

"Tell me everything."

And she did. When Addie finished, she felt as though she'd run a marathon. "He didn't care, Jonah. He talked about your death as though it didn't matter." She sat up, stared into his dark eyes. "It mattered to me. You matter, Jonah. I won't let him hurt you."

"No one is going to hurt me, Addie. And we'll get to the bottom of this. But first, maybe some pancakes?"

She couldn't help laughing at his hopeful expression. "Aren't you glad breakfast is the one meal I actually do well?"

He gestured to his injured left arm. "Just a few more days until I get this back. I'll be happy to cook then."

"And I'll be happy to eat whatever you cook. Food always tastes better when someone else makes it."

Chapter Fifteen

Halloween arrived, but Addie wasn't feeling it. Two days had passed since they discovered that poor woman at the Abernathy estate, and the police didn't have any tangible leads. She hadn't had any more dreams, but the fear and grief from the last one stayed with her.

On a positive note, her admirer had gone radio silent. No more ridiculous flowers or teddy bears appeared on her doorstep. And Jonah would get an all-clear from the ortho doctor tomorrow. Hopefully. That meant something. Addie pictured the new lingerie hidden in her drawer.

A yip dragged her back to the present. Gracey, always the first to beg for a treat, sat at her feet behind the counter, head cocked, tongue lolling from her mouth. "Is someone hungry?" At the word, Lily leaped from the dog bed, taking her place at her sister's side. A soft woof told Addie all she needed to know. "Two treats coming right up."

She reached under the counter and grabbed their treat container. Gertie, who loved the girls almost as much as Addie, insisted on supplying them with homemade doggie treats. Addie often joked she should expand the bakery to include canine treats. She tossed one of this month's version, pumpkin, to each dog. The girls caught them in mid-air and retreated to their bed to eat them. She was still grinning at their antics when the store phone rang.

"Smiling Dog Books, this is Addie. How may I help you?"

"You should really ask how you can save your friend, Ms. Foster."

A chill crept over her at the sound of the Englishman's voice.

"Wh-what do you mean?"

"Now, now, Ms. Foster, you're smarter than that. We each have something the other wants. You have the book. I have your precious detective. Shall we trade? Bring it to the Abernathy estate. Now. And don't think about telling anyone."

"Wait. How do I know you have Jonah?"

But she spoke to dead air. Her hands shook as she placed her phone on the counter. Lily, sensing her distress, got up from her bed and pressed her body into Addie's leg, whining softly.

"Think, Addie." She picked up her phone and called Jonah; straight to voicemail. She waited through his voicemail message, tears forming at the sound of his voice. He had to be okay. When the beep sounded, she struggled for calm. "Jonah, hey, it's me. Uh, please call me. As soon as you get this." She ended the call.

What to do?

There really wasn't any question. He had Jonah. She would do anything to save him. Addie grabbed her purse and keys. "Girls, be good." She ran to the front door, flipping the lock before heading out the employee exit.

She drove to her home, barely stopping the car before jumping out. Blood roared in her ears.

Please be okay, Jonah. I just found you.

Her hands shook so badly, she dropped her keys. Cursing under her breath, she grabbed them off the porch and unlocked the door. Racing into her bedroom, she grabbed the book from a box on the floor of her closet.

Addie sprinted to her car, not stopping to lock the door. Ensuring Jonah's safety was all that mattered. Scenes of their time together rolled through her mind, like an old movie. But there weren't enough. She pressed her foot down on the gas.

Normally, the passing scenery would have caught her interest. Not today. Her pulse quickened with every passing mile. *Please be okay. Please be okay.* The mantra reverberated in her head. She tried Jonah's phone once again. Right to voicemail. A moment later, Grey's face flashed on her screen. She hit decline. *'Don't tell anyone,'* may mean her BFF as well. Besides, he'd freak out when he heard what she was doing and call the police. She couldn't risk it.

The miles passed as acid swirled in her gut. The closer she got, the tighter she gripped the wheel. She loosened her hands, willing herself to relax. Breathe in. Breathe out. Repeat. Jonah needed her. Now was not the time to fall apart. That would come later.

The turn-off came before she was ready, and she took it almost on two wheels. She slowed the vehicle to give herself a moment to plan. *What?* She had no idea. She wasn't armed. And Grey, the one who practiced martial arts, was miles away.

She'd previously thought the lane, with its tunnel of trees, magnificent; now she leaned toward foreboding and gloomy. The mostly bare branches swayed in the strengthening wind. Daylight rapidly gave way to the gathering gloom. Addie shivered as she drew closer to the estate. At last, the house came into view. That, too, had changed from impressive to menacing.

She parked her car in the circle near the front door. Addie grabbed her cell, slipping it into her pocket, then the book from the passenger seat. No other cars sat in the driveway. Unsure of what to do, she walked toward the front door. It stood ajar. Just a bit. She slipped in through it.

"Hello?" she called, her voice echoing through the empty foyer. She gnawed her bottom lip and took another few steps inside. The chaotic beating of her heart roared in her ears, the only sound in the house.

Addie continued down the hallway, ending up in front of the library. Funny how she loved that room the first time she saw it; now, dread pooled in her stomach. She placed her hand against the cool wood of the door and debated entering, when she heard footsteps behind her. She felt the sharp prick on her neck before she could turn. Darkness surrounded her.

*****

Addie swam up to the surface of consciousness. Fought against the waves of nausea. She coughed into the rag tied around her face. Her head pounded. She struggled against the ropes, trying to free her hands. But all she gained were sore wrists. She glanced around the room, searching for something to help her get free.

The door to the room opened. She closed her eyes. Better to let him think that whatever he'd injected her with still affected her. Two voices reached her ears. Both so faint, she couldn't make out the words being said. But their tone sent icy shivers down her spine.

Addie risked a glance through slit eyes. The Englishman stood with his back to her, facing the open door. The other person, a female, stood just out of sight in the hallway. The woman's heels echoed, growing fainter as she left. Addie waited for the sound of the front door, but it never came.

"I know you're awake, Ms. Foster. I didn't give you that hefty of a dose."

His voice grew closer as he approached. Addie opened her eyes. He reached towards her, sliding the gag from her mouth.

"Where's Jonah? Don't hurt him. Please. I'll tell you whatever you want to hear."

"Of course you will, my dear." A chuckle - dry, as though not often used - exploded from his chest. He leaned over her, close enough that the stench of his breath sickened her. She took shallow breaths through her mouth. "I'm afraid it's too late for your friend."

Addie jack-knifed into a seated position. "What have you done to him?"

He dragged a wing chair over to within feet of her and sat. "Oh, it was quick. Don't worry."

"I don't believe you." Her racing heart contradicted her words. She couldn't lose Jonah now. Not when she'd just found him.

"Not believing me doesn't change his fate. Now, tell me about these numbers." He pointed to the old, heavy book, now lying on a table next to him. "What did you find? I watched you, the three of you, tramping around in the woods."

She remembered the disquieting feeling of being watched. "That was you?"

"Yes. From a distance, of course. What did you find?"

Addie's mouth flattened. "Why should I tell you?"

"Spunky! How very American of you." Then his eyes changed, becoming pools of darkness. "You will tell me what I want to know. How you die depends on it."

"You mean you might not strangle me like you did poor Betty?"

He flicked a hand. "Oh, I didn't mean for that to happen. Wrong place, wrong time."

Her stomach lurched at his lack of humanity. "Betty was a human being, a nice one at that. How can you be so callous?"

A queer smile lit his face. "I had nothing against her personally, but she caught me, after hours, looking through the library. Couldn't have her telling anyone, could I?"

His complete lack of remorse left her with a foul taste in her mouth. "What does that make me? Wrong place, wrong time?"

"Consider yourself collateral damage. I want what you have." The humorless smile flashed across his face again. "Had, as it were."

The sound of a heavy door closing echoed down the hallway. He stood, almost bowing to her. "You'll excuse me for a moment? Be a dear and stay out of trouble."

She held her breath until he left before breathing in deeply through her mouth. "Think, Addie, think."

He'd bound her ankles too tightly to allow for walking. Without any way of knowing how much time she had, Addie glanced around the room. Her gaze rested on the antique desk in the corner of the room. Made of gleaming Maple, she'd admired its beauty on Saturday. Now, she hoped it held the key to her freedom.

An image of Jonah, asleep in bed this morning, flashed through her mind. His dark hair mussed. Ridiculously long lashes fanned against his cheeks.

Hold on to that. He can't be dead.

Shaking her head, Addie inched her way across the floor towards the desk. Surely, one of the drawers held something she could use to free herself. The only saving grace in this madness was that he had tied her hands in front of her.

Heavy perspiration dampened her by the time she reached the desk. She opened drawers, searching their depths for anything she could use. Each sat empty. Her heart plummeted to her feet. There had to be something. Anything. Only the center drawer remained. She eased the chair to the side and slid it open. The slight groan of the old wood sounded like a gunshot in the quiet room. Her stomach churned trying to remember how much time had passed. It didn't matter; she needed to get out of here now.

Tears sprang to her eyes when she peered into the drawer. A very old but very sharp looking pair of scissors with ornate handles sat there. A letter opener with a matching handle shared the space. She grabbed the scissors. Moisture coated her palms as she sawed at the rope binding her ankles. The skin of her wrists burned, and blood oozed from several spots, but she blocked it out. Getting out of here and finding Jonah were all that mattered.

"Yes," she cried when the blade of the scissors cut through the rope at last.

She stilled, waited to see if anyone heard her, before shaking the rope off her ankles. She flexed her feet, coaxing blood flow back into them. Sharp pins and needles raced through her skin, but she ignored the feeling, pulling herself upright on the desk. She dropped into the chair and glanced at her hands. How could she get them undone? Grasping the heavy scissors in her perspiration-slicked hands, Addie struggled to hold them at the right angle to cut the rope.

"Come on, you can do this," she muttered to herself.

But her pep talk failed. The scissors dropped from her hands, clattering to the floor. Muttering something else altogether, she grabbed them and tried again. Precious seconds ticked by. Knowing she had little time left, Addie stood, shoving the scissors and letter opener in her pocket. He'd return at any moment, and she had to be somewhere else when he did. She crept to the door on wobbly legs. Once there, she pressed her ear against it, listening for any sounds from the hallway. And counted to one hundred before easing open the massive door. The hallway stood empty.

Indecision became her enemy. *What to do?* She had no idea where her cell phone or keys might be. Bolting outside to her car wasn't an option. On the other hand, she had very little working knowledge of the estate, having only been in this room and the foyer. But finding a place to hide would buy her time. Until what? Even Lassie needed a clue. How long before Grey missed her? But would he think of this place? Probably not. Dashing off without telling anyone had seemed like such a good idea.

Knowing she'd run out of time, Addie looked up and down the hallway before dashing to the foyer. Her eyes took in the grand staircase leading upstairs. Up or out? She sprinted for the door. Better to hide in the woods than stay here trapped with that madman. And maybe she could wave down a passing car for help.

A shout from the direction she just came clinched it for her. He knew she'd escaped. Addie gripped the handle with her bound hands, opening it only as far as she needed to slip through before closing it behind her. With the Englishman's angry shouts echoing behind her, she ran off the porch and sprinted towards the woods.

Chapter Sixteen

Fat, chilly raindrops landed on her face as Addie reached the trees. She couldn't get a break today. The air had chilled since her arrival. Without her phone and with whatever he'd injected her with, she had no idea of the time. She glanced up. Daylight gave over to a dark, threatening sky. But it could be five or eight for all she knew.

"There she is!" drifted across the circular drive, followed on its heels by the crack of a gunshot.

Addie ducked and plunged into the woods. Low hanging branches slapped her face, but the pain receded with her fear. She ran in the direction of the highway; at least she hoped. Pain, fear, and uncertainty clouded her mind. She really should have paid attention to those long-ago Girl Scout camping trips. Too late now.

Her sides cramped, but she kept up her pace, running with her head ducked and bound hands in front of her. She tried to remember the length of the estate driveway. Half-mile? Mile? It didn't matter. She kept running. After a few minutes, she stopped, taking shelter behind a tree. She strained to hear him, hoping against hope he hadn't followed her. She concentrated on her breathing. In. Out. Her lungs burned and ribs ached from the exertion. Addie tipped her face to the sky, catching small amounts of rain to slake her thirst. Her head ached and remained cloudy from the sedative. She shook it to clear it before moving off again. Unless her eyes deceived her, the woods ahead seemed thinner. Maybe she'd gone in the right direction after all. She tramped along, sending positive thoughts into the universe for Jonah's safety.

Please be okay. Please be okay.

The ground sloped steeply upwards. She concentrated on keeping her balance in the slippery leaves. Addie balanced herself on each tree she passed until she reached the top. A car whizzed by. Cold rain poured down. The normalcy of the scene relieved her. She'd made it. She walked to the edge of the road and then along it, facing any oncoming traffic that appeared. Someone would help her.

Minutes later, she realized this wasn't a busy stretch of road. But surely someone had to drive by. As though she conjured it, the lights of a truck shone on her as it rounded a bend.

"Hey!" she yelled, waving her bound wrists. "Please, help me." She debated running into the road but feared being struck in the gathering gloom.

Her tired body sagged as she watched it slow and pull onto the shoulder of the road. As it pulled abreast of her, the stenciled words 'Worthington Estate Sales' came into view.

"Claire!"

The passenger window lowered. "Goodness, Addie, what happened to you?" The older woman placed the pickup in park before coming around to help Addie up into the truck.

Words poured out of Addie on a sob. "Oh, Claire, I'm relieved to see you. Help me." She held out her bound wrists in front of her.

"Let's get you in the truck." She helped Addie into a sitting position, securing her seat belt around her before getting in on the other side. Pulling back onto the road, Claire glanced at Addie's wrists. "That looks painful."

"I'm not going to lie. It stings." She held up her hands. "Can you untie me?"

Instead of answering, Claire accelerated.

"Claire, did you hear me?" A sinking in her stomach answered for her.

"I never meant for anyone to get hurt. It was about the treasure. Always the treasure." She shook her head, blonde ponytail whipping around it. "It doesn't matter now." She said nothing else as she took the turn-off to the estate.

Addie shrunk away, pressing against the door. She glanced down at the passing ground. Did jumping make sense? She couldn't break her fall with her hands still tied. What if she broke her neck instead?

"I wouldn't if I were you," Claire commented as she sped up.

Her mind raced as they cleared the trees. The estate loomed ahead, chilling in the stormy sky. The pickup's headlights caught a navy-blue Jeep parked near the front door.

Grey!

Terror clawed at her throat. She didn't want her BFF getting in the middle of this.

"Expecting company?" asked Claire as she turned off the engine. And pulled a nasty looking revolver from her purse. "Another body won't matter at this point in the game." She waved the gun in her direction. "Slide across the seat towards me. No funny stuff."

Addie's head pounded trying to figure out a way out of this mess. She did as told, lowering her shaky legs to the ground. And felt the metal of the muzzle stuck into her back. Unlike the last two mysteries in her life, she'd not had a later dream to give her a hint at how this would end. Why have some weird, pseudo psychic ability if you didn't have it when needed?

"Hurry it up," Claire growled before shoving her forward.

At the same time, a huge flash of lightning, followed almost immediately by a crack of thunder, startled her. She heard Claire gasp. Without thinking, Addie turned and shoved the other woman to the ground. And then ran. This time, she chose the estate. Whipping through the door, she locked it behind her. Claire most likely had keys, but this would at least buy her a moment.

Addie ran down the darkened hallway to the only room she knew in the house. The library. She fingered the handle of the letter opener and scissors in her pocket. At least she had some sort of weapon. Although it wouldn't do much against a gun.

Reaching the library, she eased the door open, praying it wouldn't make any noise, and slipped inside. And shrieked as arms grabbed her from behind. One hand covered her mouth.

"Shhh. It's me," whispered Grey.

"It's us, actually," added Jonah.

Terror dissolved into relief. She whirled and launched herself at both men. She kissed both. Grey on the cheek. Jonah on the lips.

"He told me he'd killed you," she breathed against his lips. "I didn't believe them. Couldn't," she finished on a sob.

"Hey, I'm right here. And I'm okay. Except for the ten years you just took off my life."

"Right off the top," Grey concurred.

Jonah slid from her grasp. "I need to make a phone call. Summon the cavalry, so to speak." He pulled his cell from the back pocket of his jeans.

She turned to Grey while Jonah made the call. "How did you know I was in trouble? How did you know where to find me?"

"Well, when you didn't answer any of my calls, I knew something was up."

"You only called once. And I couldn't. He made that clear. Tell anyone, and Jonah died." She swallowed past the lump in her throat. Even knowing he stood next to her, that thought took her breath.

"No, more like a million. Check your phone."

"He took it."

"And that's the thing. You always have your phone on you. No matter what. And then the shop being closed in the middle of the day was a dead giveaway. Pardon the pun."

"Ugh, Grey, really?"

"I know. It's an illness. Anyway, I drove to the store to find this guy peeking in the windows." He pointed a thumb in Jonah's direction.

Jonah finished his call at that moment. "Help is on the way. First car should be only a few minutes out. What did I miss?" He smiled at her, running one finger along her cheek. "I got your message, but you didn't pick up when I called you back. So, I went to the store."

"Grey was just telling me how you guys found me. Go ahead, Grey."

"We went inside the shop, not at all sure what we might find."

"And what we found were two agitated Shelties behind the desk."

"Oh."

"'Oh,' she says." Grey dragged a hand through his hair.

"In my defense, I couldn't bring them with me. I had no idea what I'd find."

"Exactly," growled Jonah. He stopped right in front of her and leaned down until his face hovered mere inches from hers. "You're not trained. You're not armed. You had no idea what to expect. How could you be so foolish?"

"He told me he would kill you if I didn't bring the book," she whispered. "And you didn't answer."

His face lost its stony appearance. "Oh, Addie."

"He said to bring it and to come alone. He thr-thr-threatened to kill you if I didn't follow the directions." She blew out a big breath. "And even afterwards, he told me he'd already killed you. But I didn't believe. Couldn't believe. Not when I'd just found you."

And the fight left him. Jonah gathered him to her, resting his cheek on the crown of her head. "No one's going anywhere. I've got you."

She shivered in his arms, knowing how close she'd come to being lost. She snuggled further into him. "And I've got you."

"Hate to break this to you, kids, but there's still the matter of at least two people in this house who would rather have us dead."

Jonah leaned back enough to look into her eyes. He nodded towards Grey. "It's always going to be something with him, isn't it?"

She laughed. "Pretty much."

"He does have a point though." A sigh ripped through him. "To be continued?"

"Agreed."

He straightened and let go of her. She missed his solid warmth already. "Tell me what we're dealing with."

So, she did, including Claire's betrayal. "I just can't get over her involvement in this. Betty worked for her for years. How could she kill her?"

"People get crazy over money."

"Grey, there isn't any money. Just an old legend."

"Which means the possibility of money. Large sums of it. I asked Dan to take a closer look at the financials for Claire's family business. Not great. She's holding it together by the skin of her teeth. Desperate people do desperate things."

"Then you can understand why I have to ask Addie to come with me."

Addie gasped at Claire's voice behind them. She whirled. "Where did you come from?"

Claire reached out a hand, not the one holding the gun, and patted the paneled wall. "You have to love these old houses, with all their secret passages." She pointed the gun at Addie. "Enough chit chat. You two guys can leave. Addie, you're coming with me."

The wail of police cars permeated the room. Jonah took a step forward. "You aren't going to get away with this. You're not even going to get out of here."

"I wouldn't be so sure. Addie, you have three seconds to decide. Come with me, or I put a bullet in lover boy's brain."

There wasn't any decision to make. Addie stepped forward, coming to a halt next to her.

"No!" Jonah cried, reaching out for her.

She held up a hand to him and smiled. "It's okay. You and Grey go outside. Tell the police everything is fine in here. Claire isn't going to shoot me."

"I'm not leaving you here with her."

"Neither am I," declared Grey.

Claire grabbed Addie, pulling her back against her. She shoved the barrel of the gun in her side. "You are if you don't care to watch her die in front of you. Now, go."

"Please, guys, do what she says. I'll be okay."

Footsteps and shouts echoed in the hallway. Help had arrived. But were they too late? If only Jonah and Grey would leave. What if Claire turned the gun on one of them?

As though she could read her thoughts, Claire pulled the gun from her side, pointing it straight at Jonah. The wavering of her hand sent chills through Addie's heart. They'd run out of time.

Addie pulled the antique scissors from her pocket. Channeling all her fear and rage, she embedded them in the other woman's thigh.

And then chaos erupted. Mingled screams and a loud blast from the handgun competed for her attention. Plaster rained down from the ceiling where the stray shot had landed. A heartbeat later, the library doors burst open, uniformed officers spilling in to take custody of Claire.

But none of that mattered. The two guys she cared most about in the world stood there, unharmed. Tears streamed down her face as she hugged them both.

Chapter Seventeen

"Don't get used to this. I mean, I do make a mean omelet, but I can't be over here every morning cooking for y'all." Grey slid a portion onto each of their plates before turning to the sink to rinse the pan.

Addie grinned at her BFF's back. And the expression on Jonah's face. He seemed torn between being alone with her and the delicious aroma wafting from his plate. She decided to put him out of his misery.

"And Jonah and I certainly appreciate your cooking for us. But maybe you could go have breakfast with Jamie."

Jonah smothered a chuckle in his juice glass.

Grey dried his hands. And looked between the two of them. "Oh! I get it. You'd like to be alone. Consider me gone." He brushed a kiss on her hair and waltzed out the back door.

"I thought he'd never take the hint," Addie sighed.

Jonah took one of her hands in his. "Don't get me wrong, he's growing on me, but a little alone time works, too." He raised her hand to his lips, never dropping her gaze as he kissed it.

And the zings coursed throughout her body. "What time is your orthopedic appointment? Grey can cover while I go with you."

"Not until this afternoon." He glanced at his arm, still encased in the splint. "I'm ready to get my arm back."

She wiggled her eyebrows at him. "Me, too."

A broad smile lit his face. With a gleam in his eye, he said, "Maybe I can get them to move it up a few hours."

Addie squeezed his hand and smiled. No words necessary.

The End

Acknowledgments

With every book, I say, "Now, that's my favorite cover." Then the next one comes along. Murder by Numbers is no exception to that rule. Thank you, Rebecca Pau, for your continued ability to amaze me with your talent!!

Thank you to my amazing group of fellow writers, Tammryn, Adrienne, Carrie, Ester, Maria Elena, Victoria, Delta to name just a few. Your continued support, endless advice, and wicked humor makes my day and helps me to keep going.

To Margie Greenhow, my amazing PA. What a fun journey this has been with you. I can only imagine where the road leads.

Thank you, Karen Boston, for your brilliant editing. And humorous comments on the side. They make me giggle as I slog through the pages.

My husband, Mark, and my children, Jordan & Lucas mean the world to me. I know it's not easy when I shush you because I'm trying to write or edit or something writing related. How many soccer games have I attended with my laptop in tow? I appreciate your patience and love y'all very much.

To Melissa, Tianna, Bridget, Sara, Jimmy, and Sharon for their continued and dogged stalking of me. Did you read the dedication???

How to Help an Indie Author

Reviews, reviews, reviews! Even if you don't fall in love with my books, please take the time to review them on Amazon, Goodreads and/or Book Bub. Reviews are so much more important than you could ever imagine.

Follow me everywhere:
Facebook: https://www.facebook.com/profile.
php?id=100012114317732
Twitter: https://twitter.com/K_OMalley67
Instagram: https://www.instagram.com/kimberleyomalley67/
Amazon Author Page: www.amazon.com/author/
kimberleyomalley
Good Reads Profile: http://bit.ly/grKOM
Book Bub profile: http://bit.ly/bookbubKOM
Check out my website at www.kimberleyomalley.com

To keep up with me and my books, sign up for my newsletter:
http://eepurl.com/dgonEX

What's Next?

Addie Foster Mysteries books four, five, and six will release this summer. Here's a sneak peek of Book four, yet unnamed. Keep in mind, this book is still being written and subject to change.

Addie walked down the dimly lit hall, unsure of her surroundings. She turned her head from side to side, seeking anything familiar. Each wall held numbered doors, like a hotel or a hospital. Yet no one else appeared. She rubbed her arms despite the warmth.

"Hello?" she called out. And stopped to listen for a response. Nothing. "Where is everybody?" Again, only silence reached her ears. At the very end of the hall, faint light spilled from a cracked door. Maybe whomever she sought was in there. She made her way towards it, each step becoming more difficult. Something scared her, made her hesitate before the opened door. She leaned forward, trying to catch the voice within.

"There, there. No reason to suffer anymore. I'm here to help you ease your pain."

The words sent chills down her spine. Addie turned to flee, not wanting to know what lay within the room. A hand gripped her wrist. "Where do you think you're going?"

The chill of the hardwood floor under her back dragged Addie Foster from the nightmare's tenacious grip. She shook her head to clear it, ebony curls bouncing with the motion. And was swarmed by two excitable Shelties. Gracey and Lily washed her face with their pink tongues.

"Mom's okay, girls."

"I hoped we'd at least have a few months before this started again," groused a sleepy male voice from somewhere above her.

"It's not like I can control it," she muttered in reply. *He had a point though.*

Jonah Wolfe, her boyfriend of a few months, slid off the bed, joining her on the floor. Her took her chilled hands in his own, blowing on them. "I'm sorry. I know this is rough on you. Do you want to talk about it?"

"Not yet. Maybe over breakfast."

Gracey, the bolder of her two dogs, scratched at the closed bedroom door. She looked back at them over her shoulder as if to hurry them along.

Addie laughed. "Ah, the joys of dog ownership. Or having a girlfriend with dogs in your case."

Jonah sprang to his feet in that ridiculously athletic way he had. "My turn to make breakfast, so I'll take the girls out while I'm at it. Why don't you grab a shower? Scrambled okay with you?"

She stood, way less gracefully than he had, and stretched onto her toes to kiss his cheek. "Anything that I haven't cooked is okay with me. See you in a few." He left the room, chatting away to her little dogs. Taking a piece of her heart with him. She sighed and wondered aloud to the universe how she'd gotten so lucky. Not for the first time. Not even for the hundredth.

Twenty minutes later, the divine scent of pumpkin spiced something drew her to the kitchen. Jonah grinned over his shoulder from the stove. "How does pumpkin spiced pancakes sound?"

"Delicious," she murmured, sniffing the air. "Have I mentioned how much I love fall?"

"Only every day. I thought you loved summer the most. Didn't you tell me that when we met?"

"Interesting choice of words, Jonah." They 'met' in July, right down the block from her home. When she found a dead body. Blood soaked her clothing when they 'met.' He thought she had killed that man. "And when summer rolls around again, it will be my favorite season. Again."

"Ah. You're fickle." He leaned in as she passed, kissing her hair. "As long as your infidelity only applies to the seasons."

"Of course," she replied from within the refrigerator. She bumped the door closed with a hip and carried syrup, butter, and juice to the table.

He joined her, placing a dish covered in pancakes. "I may have made a few too many."

"What gave it away?" she asked, placing two of them on her own plate. "We really should be training for Thanksgiving."

Jonah halted his fork hallway to his mouth. "Training?"

"You've had many meals at the aunties by now. You should know better."

He dropped the fork. "More food than usual?"

"Give the man a Kewpie doll. Aunt Clementine and Aunt Beatrice use Thanksgiving as an excuse to pull out all the stops. And I mean all. There will be course after course. Thus, the need to start training now."

"And by training you mean eating less?" He glanced at his forsaken pancakes.

He looked like a small boy who'd had his favorite toy taken away from him. "Maybe after breakfast."

"Good idea. I'll get right on that." Shoving a large piece of pancake in his mouth didn't convince her of his sincerity.

"I'm not kidding. Ask Grey. Or Gertie. You can count on gaining a good five pounds between all the holiday meals."

"More of me to love," he smirked around another bite.

She threw her napkin at his head.